For the first time, as Khalis led her back to the tent and drew her down to the pillows' opulent softness, she wanted to tell the last of her secrets. She wanted to bare her soul. She wanted, Grace knew, to be understood, accepted. *Forgiven.*

Yet as Khalis bent to trail kisses from her throat to her tummy, and desire dazed her senses, Grace knew that was impossible. So she would just take this one night, this physical understanding and acceptance and pleasure, and it would have to be enough.

Khalis's mouth moved lower, his tongue flicking against her skin, and hazily she thought that it could be more than enough. Then she stopped thinking completely.

Kate Hewitt discovered her first Mills & Boon® romance on a trip to England when she was thirteen, and she's continued to read them ever since. She wrote her first story at the age of five, simply because her older brother had written one and she thought she could do it too. That story was one sentence long—fortunately they've become a bit more detailed as she's grown older. She has written plays, short stories and magazine serials for many years, but writing romance remains her first love. Besides writing, she enjoys reading, travelling and learning to knit.

After marrying the man of her dreams—her older brother's childhood friend—she lived in England for six years, and now resides in Connecticut with her husband, her three young children, and the possibility of one day getting a dog.

Kate loves to hear from readers—you can contact her through her website: www.kate-hewitt.com

Recent titles by the same author:

KHOLODOV'S LAST MISTRESS
MR AND MISCHIEF
 (The Powerful and the Pure)
BOUND TO THE GREEK

**Did you know these are also available as eBooks?
Visit www.millsandboon.co.uk**

THE DARKEST
OF SECRETS

BY
KATE HEWITT

First published in Great Britain 2012
by Mills & Boon, an imprint of Harlequin (UK) Limited.
Harlequin (UK) Limited, Eton House, 18-24 Paradise Road,
Richmond, Surrey TW9 1SR

© Kate Hewitt 2012

ISBN: 978 0 263 22717 8

Harlequin (UK) policy is to use papers that are natural, renewable and recyclable products and made from wood grown in sustainable forests. The logging and manufacturing process conform to the legal environmental regulations of the country of origin.

Printed and bound in Great Britain
by CPI Antony Rowe, Chippenham, Wiltshire

THE DARKEST
OF SECRETS

To Jennie, Natasha, and Maisey,
who encouraged me to write this book
and buy a fantastic dress in the bargain!
Thanks for all your encouragement and support.
Love, Kate.

CHAPTER ONE

'OPEN it up.'

It had taken the better part of two days to reach this moment. Khalis Tannous stood back as the two highly skilled engineers he'd employed to open his father's steel vault finally eased the door off its hinges. They had used all their knowledge and skill trying to unlock the thing, but his father was too paranoid and the security too advanced. In the end they'd had to use the newest laser technology to cut straight through the steel.

Khalis had no idea what lay inside this vault; he hadn't even known the vault had existed, on the lowest floor of the compound on his father's private island. He'd already been through the rest of the facility and found enough evidence to see his father put in prison for life, if he were still alive.

'It's dark,' one of the engineers said. They'd propped the sawn-off door against a wall and the opening to the vault was black and formless.

Khalis gave a grim smile. 'Somehow I doubt there are windows in there.' What *was* in there he couldn't even guess. Treasure or trouble? His father had had a penchant for both. 'Give me a torch,' he said, and one was passed into his hand.

He flicked it on, took a step towards the darkness. He

could feel his hand slick on the torch, his heart beating far too hard. He was scared, which annoyed him, but then he knew enough about his father to brace himself for yet another tragic testament to the man's power and cruelty.

Another step, and the darkness enveloped him like velvet. He felt a thick carpet under his feet, breathed in the surprising scents of wood and furniture polish, and felt a flicker of relief—and curiosity. He lifted the torch and shone it around the vault. It was a surprisingly large space and fashioned like a gentleman's study, with elegant sofas and chairs, even a drinks table.

Yet somehow Khalis didn't think his father came down to a sealed underground vault just to relax with a tumbler of his best single malt. He saw a switch on the wall and flicked it on, bathing the room in electric light. His torch lay forgotten in his hand as he slowly turned in a circle, gazing first at the furniture and then at the walls.

And what they held…frame after frame, canvas after canvas. Some he recognised, others he didn't but he could guess. Khalis gazed at them all, felt a heaviness settle on him like a shroud. Yet another complication. Another testament to his father's many illegal activities.

'Mr Tannous?' one of the engineers asked uneasily from the outside hallway. Khalis knew his silence had gone on too long.

'It's fine,' he called back, even though it wasn't fine at all. It was amazing…and terrible. He stepped further into the room and saw another wood-panelled door in the back. With a flicker of foreboding, he went to it. It opened easily and he entered another smaller room. Only two paintings were in this tiny chamber, two paintings that made Khalis squint and step closer. If they were what he thought they were…

'Khalis?' his assistant, Eric, called, and Khalis came

out of the little room and closed the door. He switched off the light and stepped out of the vault. The two engineers and Eric all waited, their expressions both curious and concerned.

'Leave it,' he told the engineers, who had propped the enormous steel door against the wall. He felt the beginnings of a headache and gave a brisk nod. 'I'll deal with all this later.'

No one asked any questions, which was good since he had no intention of spreading the news of what was in that vault. He didn't yet trust the skeleton staff left on the compound since his father's death, all of them now in his employ. Anyone who had worked for his father had to be either desperate or completely without scruples. Neither option inspired trust. He nodded towards the engineers. 'You can go now. The helicopter will take you to Taormina.'

They nodded, and after Khalis disarmed the security system everyone headed into the lift that led to the floors above ground. Khalis felt tension snap through his body, but then he'd been tense for a week, ever since he'd left San Francisco for this godforsaken island, when he'd learned his father and brother had both died in a helicopter crash.

He hadn't seen either of them in fifteen years, hadn't had anything to do with Tannous Enterprises, his father's dynastic business empire. It was huge, powerful and corrupt to its core...and it was now in Khalis's possession. Considering his father had disowned him quite publicly when he'd walked away from it all at the age of twenty-one, his inheritance had come as a bit of a surprise.

Back in his father's office, which he'd now taken for his own, he let out a long, slow breath and raked his hands through his hair as he considered that vault. He'd spent the last week trying to familiarise himself with his father's many assets, and then attempt to determine just how illegal they were. The vault and its contents was yet another complication in this sprawling mess.

Outside, the Mediterranean Sea sparkled jewel-bright under a lemon sun, but the island felt far from a paradise to Khalis. It had been his childhood home, but it now felt like a prison. It wasn't the high walls topped with barbed wire and broken glass that entrapped him, but his memories. The disillusionment and despair he'd felt corroding his own soul, forcing him to leave. If he closed his eyes, he could picture Jamilah on the beach, her dark hair whipping around her face as she watched him leave for the last time, her aching heart reflected in her dark eyes.

Don't leave me here, Khalis.

I'll come back. I'll come back and save you from this place, Jamilah. I promise.

He pushed the memory away, as he had been doing for the last fifteen years. *Don't look back. Don't regret or even remember.* He'd made the only choice he could; he just hadn't foreseen the consequences.

'Khalis?'

Eric shut the door and waited for instructions. In his board shorts and T-shirt, he looked every inch the California beach bum, even here on Alhaja. His relaxed outfit and attitude hid a razor-sharp mind and an expertise in computers that rivalled Khalis's own.

'We need to fly an art appraiser out here as soon as possible,' Khalis said. 'Only the best, preferably someone with a specialisation in Renaissance paintings.'

Eric raised his eyebrows, looking both intrigued and impressed. 'What are you saying? The vault had *paintings*?'

'Yes. A lot of paintings. Paintings I think could be worth millions.' He sank into the chair behind his father's desk, gazed unseeingly at the list of assets he'd been going through. Real estate, technology, finance, politics. Tannous Enterprises had a dirty finger in every pie. How, Khalis wondered, not for the first time, did you take the reins of a company that was more feared than revered, and turn it into something honest? Something good?

You couldn't. He didn't even want to.

'Khalis?' Eric prompted.

'Contact an appraiser, fly him out here. Discreetly.'

'No problem. What are you going to do with the paintings once they're appraised?'

Khalis smiled grimly. 'Get rid of them.' He didn't want anything of his father's, and certainly not some priceless artwork that was undoubtedly stolen. 'And inform the law once we know what we're dealing with,' he added. 'Before we have Interpol crawling all over this place.'

Eric whistled softly. 'This is one hell of a mess, isn't it?'

Khalis pulled a sheaf of papers towards him. 'That,' he told his assistant and best friend, 'is a complete understatement.'

'I'll get on to the appraiser.'

'Good. The sooner the better—that open vault presents too much risk.'

'You don't actually think someone is going to steal something?' Eric asked, eyebrows raised. 'Where would they go?'

Khalis shrugged. 'People can be sly and deceptive. And I don't trust anyone.'

Eric gazed at him for a moment, his blue eyes narrowed shrewdly. 'This place really did a number on you, didn't it?'

Khalis just shrugged again. 'It was home,' he said, and turned back to his work. A few seconds later he heard the door click shut.

* * *

'Special project for La Gioconda.'

'So amusing,' Grace Turner said dryly. She swivelled in her chair to glance at David Sparling, her colleague at Axis Art Insurers and one of the world's top experts on Picasso forgeries. 'What is it?' she asked as he dangled a piece of paper in front of her eyes. She refused to attempt to snatch it. She smiled coolly instead, eyebrows raised.

'Ah, there's the smile,' David said, grinning himself. Grace had been dubbed La Gioconda—the Mona Lisa—when she'd first started at Axis, both for her cool smile and her expertise in Renaissance art. 'Urgent request came in to appraise a private collection. They want a specialist in Renaissance.'

'Really?' Her curiosity was piqued in spite of her determination to remain unmoved, or at least appear so.

'Really,' David said. He dangled the paper a bit closer. 'Aren't you just a teeny bit curious, Grace?'

Grace swivelled back to her computer and stared at the appraisal she'd been working on for a client's seventeenth century copy of a Caravaggio. It was good, but not that good. It wouldn't sell for as much as he'd hoped. 'No.'

David chuckled. 'Even when I tell you they'll fly the appraiser out to some private island in the Mediterranean, all expenses paid?'

'Naturally.' Private collections couldn't be moved easily. And most people were very private about their art. She paused, her fingers hovering over the keys of her computer. 'Do you know the collector?' There were only a handful of people in the entire world who owned significant collections of Renaissance paintings of real value, and most of them were extremely discreet…so discreet they didn't want appraisers or insurers looking in and seeing just what kind of art they had on their walls.

David shook his head. 'Too top secret for me. The boss wants to see you about it ASAP.'

'Why didn't you tell me?' she asked, and David just grinned. Pressing her lips together, she grabbed the print-out he'd been teasing her with and strode towards the office of Michel Latour, the CEO of Axis Art Insurers, her father's oldest friend and one of the most powerful men in the art world.

'You wanted to see me?'

Michel turned from the window that overlooked the Rue St Honoré in the 1st arrondissement of Paris. 'Close the door.' Grace obeyed and waited. 'You received the message?'

'A private collection with significant art from the Renaissance period to be appraised.' She shook her head slowly. 'I can think of less than half a dozen collectors who fit that description.'

'This is different.'

'How?'

Michel gave her a thin-lipped smile. 'Tannous.'

'Tannous?' She stared at him, disbelieving, her jaw dropping before she thought to snap it shut. 'Balkri Tannous?' Immoral—or perhaps amoral—businessman, and thought to be an obsessive art collector. No one knew what his art collection contained, or if it even existed. No one had ever seen it or even spoke of it. And yet the rumours flew every time a museum experienced a theft: a Klimt disappeared from a gallery in Boston, a Monet from the Louvre. Shocking, inexplicable, and yet the name Tannous was always darkly whispered around such heists. 'Wait,' Grace said slowly. 'Isn't he dead?'

'He died last week in a helicopter crash,' Michel confirmed. 'Suspicious, apparently. His son is making the enquiry.'

'I thought his son died in the crash.'

'His other son.'

Grace was silent. She had not known there was another son. 'Do you think he wants to sell the collection?' she finally asked.

'I'm not sure what he wants.' Michel moved to his desk, where a file folder lay open. He flipped through a few papers; Grace saw some scrawled notes about various heists. Tannous suspected behind every one, though no one could prove it.

'If he wanted to sell on the black market, he wouldn't have come to us.' There were plenty of shady appraisers who dealt in stolen goods and Axis was most assuredly not one of them.

'No,' Michel agreed thoughtfully. 'I do not think he intends to sell the collection on the black market.'

'You think he's going to donate it?' Grace heard the disbelief in her voice. 'The whole collection could be worth millions. Maybe even a billion dollars.'

'I don't think he needs money.'

'It doesn't have to be about need.' Michel just cocked his head, his lips curving in a half-smile. 'Who is he? I didn't even know Tannous had a second son.'

'You wouldn't. He left the Tannous fold when he was only twenty-one, after graduating from Cambridge with a First in mathematics. Started his own IT business in the States, and never looked back.'

'And his business in the U.S.? It's legitimate?'

'It appears to be.' He paused. 'The request is fairly urgent. He wishes the collection to be dealt with as soon as possible.'

'Why?'

'I can certainly appreciate why an honest businessman

would want to legally off-load a whole lot of stolen art quite quickly.'

'If he is honest.'

Michel shook his head, although there was a flicker of sympathy in his shrewd grey eyes. 'Cynicism doesn't suit you, Grace.'

'Neither did innocence.' She turned away, her mind roiling from Michel's revelations.

'You know you want to see what's in that vault,' Michel said softly.

Grace didn't answer for a moment. She couldn't deny the fact that she was curious, but she'd experienced and suffered too much not to hesitate. Resist. Temptation came in too many forms. 'He could just turn it all over to the police.'

'He might do so, after it's been appraised.'

'If it's a large collection, an appraisal could take months.'

'A proper one,' Michel agreed. 'But I believe he simply wants an experienced eye cast over the collection. It will have to be moved eventually.'

She shook her head. 'I don't like it. You don't know anything about this man.'

'I trust him,' Michel said simply. 'And I trust the fact that he went to the most legitimate source he could for appraisal.'

Grace said nothing. She didn't trust this Tannous man; of course she didn't. She didn't trust men full stop, and especially not wealthy and possibly corrupt tycoons. 'In any case,' Michel continued in that same mild tone, 'he wants the appraiser to fly to Alhaja Island—tonight.'

'Tonight?' Grace stared at her boss, mentor and one-time saviour. 'Why the rush?'

'Why not? I told you, holding onto all that art has to be an unappealing prospect. People are easily tempted.'

'I know,' Grace said softly, and regret flashed briefly in Michel's eyes.

'I didn't mean—'

'I know,' she said again, then shook her head. That brief flare of curiosity died out by decision. 'It's not something I can be involved with, Michel.' She took a deep breath, felt it sear her lungs. 'You know how careful I have to be.'

His eyes narrowed, mouth thinning. 'How long are you going to live your life enslaved to that—?'

'As long as I have to.' She turned away, not wanting Michel to see her expression, the pain she still couldn't hide, not even after four years. She was known by her colleagues to be cool, emotionless even, but it was no more than a carefully managed mask. Just thinking about Katerina made tears rise to her eyes and her soul twist inside her.

'Oh, *chérie*.' Michel sighed and glanced again at the file. 'I think this could be good for you.'

'*Good* for me—'

'Yes. You've been living your life like a church mouse, or a nun, I don't know which. Perhaps both.'

'Interesting analogies,' Grace said with a small smile. 'But I need to live a quiet life. You know that.'

'I know that you are my most experienced appraiser of Renaissance art, and I need you to fly to Alhaja Island— tonight.'

She turned to stare at him, saw the iron in his eyes. He wasn't going to back down. 'I can't—'

'You can, and you will. I might have been your father's oldest friend, but I am also your employer. I don't do favours, Grace. Not for you. Not for anyone.'

She knew that wasn't true. He'd done her a huge favour four years ago, when she'd been desperate and dying inside. When he'd offered her a job at Axis he had, in his own way, given her life again—or as much life as she could have, given her circumstances. 'You could go yourself,' she pointed out.

'I don't have the knowledge of that period that you do.'

'Michel—'

'I mean it, Grace.'

She swallowed. She could feel her heart beating inside her far too hard. 'If Loukas finds out—'

'What? You're just doing your job. Even he allows you that.'

'Still.' Nervously, she pleated her fingers together. She knew how high-octane the art world could be. Dealing with some of the finest and most expensive art in the world ignited people's passions—and possessiveness. She'd seen how a beautiful picture could poison desire, turn love into hate and beauty into ugliness. She'd lived it, and never wanted to again.

'It will all be very discreet, very safe. There's no reason for anyone even to know you are there.'

Alone on an island with the forgotten son of a corrupt and hated business tycoon? She didn't know much about Balkri Tannous, but she knew his type. She knew how ruthless, cruel and downright dangerous such a man could be. And she had no reason—yet—to believe his son would be any different.

'There will be a staff,' Michel reminded her. 'It's not as if you'd be completely alone.'

'I know that.' She took a deep breath and let it out slowly. 'How long would it take?'

'A week? It depends on what is required.'

'A *week*—'

'Enough.' Michel held up one hand. 'Enough. You will go. I insist on it, Grace. Your plane leaves in three hours.'

'Three hours? But I haven't even packed—'

'You have time.' He smiled, although his expression remained iron-like and shrewd. 'Don't forget a swimming costume. I hear the Mediterranean's nice this time of year. Khalis Tannous might give you some time off to swim.'

Khalis Tannous. The name sent a shiver of something—curiosity? Fear?—through her. What kind of man was he, the son of an undoubtedly unscrupulous or even evil man, yet who had chosen—either out of defiance or desperation—to go his own way at only twenty-one years old? And now that he was back, in control of an empire, what kind of man would he become?

'I don't intend to swim,' she said shortly. 'I intend to do the job as quickly as possible.'

'Well,' Michel said, smiling, 'you could try to enjoy yourself—for once.'

Grace just shook her head. She knew where that led, and she had no intention of *enjoying herself* ever again.

CHAPTER TWO

'THERE it is.'

Grace craned her neck to look out of the window of the helicopter that had picked her up in Sicily and was now taking her to Alhaja Island, no more than a rocky crescent-shaped speck in the distance, off the coast of Tunisia. She swallowed, discreetly wiped her hands along the sides of her beige silk trench coat and tried to staunch the flutter of nerves in her middle.

'Another ten minutes,' the pilot told her, and Grace leaned back in her seat, the whine of the propeller blades loud in her ears. She was uncomfortably aware that two of Khalis Tannous's family members had died in a helicopter crash just a little over a week ago, over these very waters. She did not wish to experience the same fate.

The pilot must have sensed something of her disquiet, for he glanced over at her and gave her what Grace supposed was meant to be a reassuring smile. 'Don't worry. It is very safe.'

'Right.' Grace closed her eyes as she felt the helicopter start to dip down. She might be one of the foremost appraisers of Renaissance art in Europe, but this was still far out of her professional experience. She mostly dealt with museums, inspecting and insuring paintings that hung on revered walls around the world. Her job took her to quiet back rooms and sterile laboratories, out of the public eye and away from scandal. Michel himself handled many private collections, dealt with the tricky and often tempestuous personalities that accompanied so much priceless art.

Yet this time he'd sent her. She opened her eyes, saw the ground seeming to swoop towards them. A strip of white sand beach, a rocky cove, a tangle of trees and, most noticeably of all, a high chain-link fence topped with two spiky strands of barbed wire and bits of broken glass. And Grace suspected that was the least of Tannous's security.

The helicopter touched down on the landing pad, where a black Jeep was already waiting. Her heart still thudding, Grace stepped out onto the tarmac. A slim man in a tie-dyed T-shirt and cut-off jeans stood there, his fair hair blowing in the sea breeze.

'Ms Turner? I'm Eric Poulson, assistant to Khalis Tannous. Welcome to Alhaja.'

Grace just nodded. He didn't look like what she'd expected, although she hadn't really thought of what a Tannous employee would look like. Certainly not a beach bum. He led her to the waiting Jeep, tossing her case in the back.

'Mr Tannous is expecting me?'

'Yes, you can refresh yourself and relax for a bit and he'll join you shortly.'

She prickled instinctively. She hated being told what to do. 'I thought this was urgent.'

He gave her a laughing glance. 'We're on a Mediterranean island, Ms Turner. What does urgent even mean?'

Grace frowned and said nothing. She didn't like the man's attitude. It was far from professional, and that was what she needed to be—always. Professional. Discreet.

Eric drove the Jeep down a pebbly road to the compound's main gates, a pair of armoured doors that looked incredibly forbidding. They opened seamlessly and silently and swung just as quietly shut behind the Jeep, yet Grace still felt them clang through her. Eric seemed relaxed, but then he obviously knew the security codes to those gates. She didn't. She had just become a prisoner. *Again.* Her heart raced and her palms dampened as nausea churned along with the memories inside her. Memories of feeling like a prisoner. *Being* a prisoner.

Why had she agreed to this?

Not just because Michel had insisted, she knew. Despite his tough talk, she could have refused. She didn't think Michel would actually fire her. No, she'd agreed because the desire to see Tannous's art collection—and see it, God willing, restored to museums—had been too strong to ignore. A temptation too great to resist.

And temptation was, unfortunately, something she knew all about.

As Grace slid out of the Jeep, she looked around slowly. The compound was an ugly thing of concrete, like a huge bunker, but the gardens surrounding it were lovely and lush, and she inhaled the scent of bougainvillea on the balmy air.

Eric led her towards the front doors of the building and disarmed yet another fingerprint-activated security system. Grace followed him into a huge foyer tiled in terracotta, a soaring skylight above, and then into a living room decorated with casual elegance, sofas and chairs in soothing neutral shades, a few well placed antiques and a view through the one-way window of the startling sweep of sea.

'May I offer you something to drink?' Eric asked, his hands dug into the pockets of his cut-off jeans. 'Juice, wine, a pina colada?'

Grace wondered if he was amused by her buttoned-up attitude. Well, she had no intention of relaxing. 'A glass of sparkling water, please.'

'Sure thing.' He left her alone, and Grace slowly circled the room. She summed up the antiques and artwork with a practised eye: all good copies, but essentially fakes. Eric returned with her water and withdrew again, promising that Tannous would be with her in a few minutes and she could just 'go ahead and relax'. *No, thanks.* Grace took a sip, frowning as the minutes ticked on. If Tannous's request really was urgent, why was he keeping her waiting like this? Was it on purpose?

She didn't like it, but then she didn't like anything about being here. Not the walls, not the armoured gates, not the man she was meant to meet. All of it brought back too many painful memories, like knives digging into her skull. What didn't kill you was meant to make you stronger, wasn't it? Grace smiled grimly. Then she must be awfully strong. Except she didn't feel strong right now. She felt vulnerable and even exposed, and that made her tense. She worked hard to cultivate a cool, professional demeanour, and just the nature of this place was causing it to crack.

She could not allow that to happen. Quickly she went to the door and tried the handle. With a shuddering rush of relief she felt it open easily. Clearly she was acting a little paranoid. She stepped out into the empty entry hall and saw a pair of French windows at the back that led to an enclosed courtyard, and an infinity pool shaded by palms shimmering in the dusky light.

Grace slipped outside, breathing in the scents of lavender and rosemary as a dry breeze rustled the hair at the nape of her neck. She brushed a tendril away from her face, tucking it back into her professional chignon, and headed towards the pool, her heels clicking on the tiles. She could hear the water in the pool slapping against the sides, the steady sound of limbs cutting through water. Someone was swimming out here in the twilight, and she thought she knew who it was.

She came around a palm tree into the pool area and saw a man cutting through the water with sinuous ease. Even swimming he looked assured. Arrogant and utterly confident in his domain.

Khalis Tannous.

A dart of irritation—no, anger—shot through her. While she was cooling her heels, anxious and tense, he was *swimming*? It felt like the most obvious kind of power play. Deliberately Grace walked to the chaise where a towel had been tossed. She picked it up, then crossed over to where Khalis Tannous was finishing his lap, her four-inch heels surely in his line of vision.

He came to the edge, long lean fingers curling around the slick tile as he glanced upwards. Grace was not prepared for the jolt of—what? Alarm? Awareness? She could not even say, but something in her sizzled to life as she gazed down into those grey-green eyes, long dark lashes spiky with water. It terrified her, and she instantly suppressed it as she coolly handed him the towel.

'Mr Tannous?'

His mouth twisted in bemusement but she took in the narrowing of his eyes, the flickering of suspicion. He was on his guard, just as she was. He hoisted himself up onto the tiles in one fluid movement and took the towel from her. 'Thank you.' He dried himself off with deliberate ease, and Grace could not keep her gaze from flicking downwards to the lean chest and lithe torso, muscled yet trim, his golden-brown skin now flecked with droplets of water. Tannous had a Tunisian father and a French mother, Grace knew, and his mixed ethnicity was evident in his unique colouring. He was beautiful, all burnished skin and sleek, powerful muscle. He gave off an aura of power, not from size, although he was tall, but from the whipcord strength and energy he exuded in every easy yet precise movement.

'And you are?' he finally said, and Grace jerked her gaze upwards.

'Grace Turner of Axis Art Insurers.' She reached in the pocket of her coat for her business card and handed it to him. He took it without looking. 'I believe you were expecting me.'

'So I was.' He slung the towel around his hips, his shrewd gaze flicking over her in one quick yet thorough assessment.

'I thought,' Grace said, keeping her voice professionally level, 'this appraisal was urgent?'

'Fairly urgent,' Tannous agreed. She said nothing, but something of her censure must have been evident for he smiled and said, 'I must apologise for what appears to have been discourtesy. I assumed the appraiser would wish to refresh himself before meeting me, and I would have time to finish my swim.'

'Herself,' Grace corrected coolly, 'and, I assure you, I am ready to work.'

'Glad to hear it, Miss—' he glanced down at her card, his eyebrows arching as he corrected himself '—*Ms* Turner.' He looked up, his gaze assessing once more, although whether he was measuring her as a woman or a professional Grace couldn't tell. She kept her gaze level. 'If you care to follow me, I'll take you to my office and we can discuss what you've come here for.'

Nodding her acceptance, Grace followed him through the pool area to a discreet door in the corner. They walked down another long hallway, the windows' shutters open to the fading sunlight still bathing the courtyard in gold, and then into a large masculine office with tinted windows overlooking the landscaped gardens on the other side of the compound.

Unthinkingly Grace walked to the window, pressed one hand against the cool glass as she gazed at all that managed beauty kept behind those high walls, the jagged bits of glass on top glinting in the last of the sun's rays. The feeling of being trapped clutched at her, made her throat close up. She forced herself to breathe evenly.

Khalis Tannous came to stand behind her and she was uncomfortably aware of his presence, and the fact that all he wore was a pair of swimming trunks and a towel. She could hear the soft sound of his breathing, feel the heat of him, and she tensed, every nerve on high alert and singing with an awareness she definitely did not want to feel.

'Very beautiful, don't you think?' he murmured and Grace forced herself not to move, not to respond in any way to his nearness.

'I find the wall quite ruins the view,' she replied and turned away from the window. Her shoulder brushed against his chest, a few water droplets clinging to the silk of her blouse. Tension twanged through her again so she felt as if she might snap. She could not deny the physical response she had to this man, but she could suppress it. Completely. Her body stiff, her head held high, she moved past him into the centre of the room.

Tannous gazed at her, his expression turning thoughtful. 'I quite agree with your assessment,' he said softly. She did not reply. 'I'll just get dressed,' he told her, and disappeared through another door tucked in the corner of the room.

Grace took a deep breath and let it out slowly. She could handle this. She was a professional. She'd concentrate on her job and forget about the man, the memories. For being in this glorified prison certainly brought back the memories of another island, another wall. And all the heartbreak that had followed—of her own making.

'Ms Turner.'

Grace turned and saw Tannous standing in the doorway. He had changed into a pewter-grey silk shirt, open at the throat, and a pair of black trousers. He'd looked amazing in nothing but a towel, but he looked even better in these casually elegant clothes, his lean strength powerfully apparent in every restrained movement, the silk rippling over his muscled body. She took a slight step backwards.

'Mr Tannous.'

'Please, call me Khalis.' Grace said nothing. He smiled faintly. 'Tell me about yourself, Ms Turner. You are, I take it, experienced in the appraisal of Renaissance art?'

'It is my speciality, Mr Tannous.'

'Khalis.' He sat behind the huge oak desk, steepling his fingers under his chin, clearly waiting for her to continue.

'I have a PhD in seventeenth century da Vinci copies.'

'Forgeries.'

'Yes.'

'I don't think you will be dealing with forgeries here.'

A leap of excitement pulsed through her. Despite her alarm and anxiety about being in this place, she really did want to see what was in that vault. 'If you'd like to show me what you wish to be appraised—'

'How long have you been with Axis Art Insurers?'

'Four years.'

'You are, I must confess, very young to be so experienced.'

Grace stifled a surge of annoyance. She was, unfortunately, used to clients—mainly men—casting doubt upon her abilities. Clearly Khalis Tannous was no different. 'Monsieur Latour can vouch for my abilities, Mr Tannous—'

'Khalis,' he said softly.

Awareness rippled over her in a shiver, like droplets of water on bare skin. She didn't want to call him by his first name, as ridiculous as that seemed. Keeping formal would be one way of maintaining a necessary and professional distance. 'If you'd prefer another appraiser, please simply say so. I will be happy to oblige you.' Leaving this island—and all the memories it churned up—would be a personal relief, if a professional disappointment.

He smiled, seeming so very relaxed. 'Not at all, Ms Turner. I was simply making an observation.'

'I see.' She waited, wary, tense, trying to look as unconcerned as he did. He didn't speak, and impatience bit at her. 'So the collection…?' she finally prompted.

'Ah, yes. The collection.' He turned to stare out of the window, his easy expression suddenly turning guarded, hooded. He seemed so urbane and assured, yet for just a moment he looked like a man in the grip of some terrible force, in the cast of an awful shadow. Then his face cleared and he turned back to her with a small smile. 'My father had a private collection of art in the basement of this compound. A collection I knew nothing about.' Grace refrained from comment. Tannous arched one eyebrow in gentle mockery. 'You doubt me.'

Of course she did. 'I am not here to make judgements, Mr Tannous.'

'Are you ever,' he mused, 'going to call me Khalis?'

Not if she could help it. 'I prefer work relationships to remain professional.'

'And calling me by my first name is too intimate?' There was a soft, seductive lilt to his voice that made that alarming awareness creep along Grace's spine and curl her toes. The effect this man had on her—his voice, his smile, his body—was annoying. Unwanted. She smiled tightly.

'*Intimate* is not the word I would use. But if you feel as strongly about it as you seem to, then I'm happy to oblige you and call you Khalis.' Her tongue seemed to tangle itself on his name, and her voice turned breathy. Grace inwardly flinched. She was making a fool of herself and yet, even so, she'd seen something flare in his eyes, like silver fire, when she said his name. Whatever she was feeling—this attraction, this magnetism—he felt it, too.

Not that it mattered. Attraction, to her, was as suicidal as a moth to a flame. 'May I see the paintings?' she asked.

'Of course. Perhaps that will explain things.'

In one fluid movement Khalis rose from the desk and walked out of the study, clearly expecting Grace to follow him. She suppressed the bite of irritation she felt at his arrogant attitude—he didn't even look back—only to skid to a surprised halt when she saw him holding the door open for her.

He smiled down at her, and Grace had the uncomfortable feeling that he knew exactly what she'd been feeling. 'After you,' he murmured and, fighting a flush, she walked past him down the same corridor they had used earlier. 'Where am I going?' she asked tersely. She could *feel* Khalis walking behind her, heard the whisper of his clothes as he moved. Everything about him was elegant, graceful and sinuous. Sexy.

No. She could not—would not—think that way. She hadn't looked at a man in a sexual or romantic way in four years. She'd trained herself not to, suppressed those longings because she'd had to. One misstep would cost her if not her life, then her very soul. It was insane to feel anything now—and especially for a man like Khalis Tannous, a man who was now the CEO of a terrible and corrupt empire, a man she could never trust.

Instinctively she walked a little faster, as if she could distance herself from him, but he kept pace with ease.

'Turn right,' he murmured, and she heard humour in his voice. 'You are amazingly adept in those very high heels, Ms Turner. But it's not a race.'

Grace didn't answer, but she forced herself to slow down. A little. She turned and walked down another long corridor, the shutters open to a different side of the villa's interior courtyard.

'And now left,' he said, his voice a soft caress, raising the tiny hairs on the back of Grace's neck. He'd come close again, too close. She turned left and came to a forbidding-looking lift with steel doors and a complex security pad.

Khalis activated the security with a fingerprint and a numbered code while Grace averted her eyes. 'I'll have to give you access,' he said, 'as all the art will need to stay on the basement level.'

'To be honest, Mr Tannous—'

'Khalis.'

'I'm not sure how much can be accomplished here,' Grace continued, undeterred. 'Most appraisals need to be done in a laboratory, with the proper equipment—'

Khalis flashed her a quick and rather grim smile. 'It appears my father had the same concerns you do, Ms Turner. I think you will find all the equipment and tools you need.'

The lift doors opened and Khalis ushered her inside before stepping into the lift himself. The doors swooshed closed, and Grace fought a sudden sense of claustrophobia. The lift was spacious enough, and there were only two of them in there, but she still felt as if she couldn't breathe. Couldn't think. She was conscious of Khalis next to her, seeming so loose-limbed and relaxed, and the lift plunging downwards, deep below the earth, to the evil heart of this awful compound. She felt both trapped and tempted— two things she hated feeling.

'Just a few more seconds,' Khalis said softly, and she knew he was aware of how she felt. She was used to hiding her emotions, and being good at it, and it amazed and alarmed her that this stranger seemed to read her so quickly and easily. No one else ever had.

The doors opened and he swept out one arm, indicating she could go first. Cautiously Grace stepped out into a nondescript hallway, the concrete floor and walls the same as those in any basement. To the right she saw a thick steel door, sawn off its hinges and now propped to the side. Balkri Tannous's vault. Her heart began to beat with heavy thuds of anticipation and a little fear.

'Here we are.' Khalis moved past her to switch on the light. Grace saw the interior of the vault was fashioned like a living room or study and, with her heart still beating hard, she stepped into that secret room.

It was almost too much to take in at once. Paintings jostled for space on every wall, frames nearly touching each other. She recognised at least a dozen stolen paintings right off the bat—Klimt, Monet, Picasso. Millions and millions of dollars' worth of stolen art.

Her breath came out in a shudder and Khalis laughed softly, the sound somehow bleak. 'I'm no expert, but even I could tell this was something else.'

She stopped in front of a Picasso that hadn't been seen in a museum in over twenty years. She wasn't that experienced with contemporary art, but she doubted it was a forgery. 'Why,' she asked, studying the painting's clean geometric shape and different shades of blue, 'did you ask for a Renaissance expert? There's art from every period here.'

'True,' Khalis said. He came to stand by her shoulder, gazing at the Picasso as well. 'Although, frankly, that looks like something my five-year-old god-daughter might paint in Nursery.'

'That's enough to make Picasso roll in his grave.'

'Well, she is very clever.'

Grace gave a little laugh, surprising herself. She rarely laughed. She rarely let a man make her laugh. 'Is your god-daughter in California?'

'Yes, she's the daughter of one of my shareholders.'

Grace gazed at the painting. 'Clever she may be, but most art historians would shudder to compare Picasso with a child and a box of finger paints.'

'Oh, she has a paintbrush.'

Grace laughed again, softly, a little breath of sound. 'Maybe she'll be famous one day.' She half-turned and, with a somersault of her heart, realised just how close he had come. His face—his *lips*—were mere inches away. She could see their mobile fullness, amazed at how such a masculine man could have such lush, kissable, *sexy* lips. She felt a shaft of longing pierce her and quickly she moved onto the next painting. 'So why me? Why a Renaissance specialist?'

'Because of these.'

He took her hand in his own and shock jolted through her with the force of an electric current, short-circuiting her senses. Grace jerked her hand away from his too hard, her breath coming out in an outraged gasp.

Khalis stopped, an eyebrow arched. Grace knew her reaction had been ridiculously extreme. How could she explain it? She could not, not easily at any rate. She decided to ignore the whole sorry little episode and raised her chin a notch. 'Show me, please.'

'Very well.' With one last considering look he led her

to a door she hadn't noticed in the back of the room. He opened it and switched on an electric light before ushering her inside.

The room was small and round, and it felt like being inside a tower, or perhaps a shrine. Grace saw only two artworks on the walls, and they stole the breath right from her lungs.

'What—' She stepped closer, stared hard at the wood panels with their thick brushstrokes of oil paint. 'Do you know what these are?' she whispered.

'Not precisely,' Khalis told her, 'but they definitely aren't something my god-daughter could paint.'

Grace smiled and shook her head. 'No, indeed.' She stepped closer, her gaze roving over the painted wood panels. 'Leonardo da Vinci.'

'Yes, he's quite famous, isn't he?'

Her smile widened, to her own amazement. She hadn't expected Khalis Tannous to *amuse* her. 'He is, rather. But they could be forgeries, you know.'

'I doubt they are,' Khalis answered. 'Simply by the fact they're in their own little room.' He paused, his tone turning grim. 'And I know my father. He didn't like to be tricked.'

'Forgeries can be of exceptional quality,' Grace told him. 'And they even have their own value—'

'My father—' Khalis cut her off '—liked the best.'

She turned back to the paintings, drinking them in. If these were real…how many people had seen these *ever*? 'How on earth did he find them?'

'I have no idea. I don't really want to know.'

'They weren't stolen, at least not from a museum.'

'No?'

'These have never been in a museum.'

'Then they are rather special, aren't they?'

She gave a little laugh. 'You could say that.' She shook her head slowly, still trying to take it in. Two original Leonardo paintings never seen in a museum. Never known to exist, beyond rumours. 'If these are real, they would comprise the most significant find of the art world in the last century.'

Khalis sighed heavily, almost as if he were disappointed by such news. 'I suspected as much,' he said, and flicked out the lights. 'You can examine them at length later. But right now I think we both deserve some refreshment.'

Her mind still spinning, Grace barely took in his words. 'Refreshment?'

'Dinner, Ms Turner. I'm starving.' And with an almost wolfish smile he led her out of the vault.

CHAPTER THREE

GRACE paced the sumptuous bedroom Eric had shown her to, her mind still racing from the revelations found in that vault. She longed to ring Michel, but she'd discovered her mobile phone didn't get reception on this godforsaken island. She wondered if that was intentional; somehow she didn't think Balkri Tannous wanted his guests having free contact with the outside world. But what about Khalis?

It occurred to her, not for the first time but with more force, that she really knew nothing about this man. Michel had given her the barest details: he was Balkri Tannous's younger son; he'd gone to Cambridge; he'd left his family at twenty-one and made his own way in America. But beyond that?

She knew he was handsome and charismatic and arrogantly assured. She knew his closeness made her heart skip a beat. She knew the scent and heat of him had made her dizzy. He'd made her laugh.

Appalled by the nature of her thoughts, Grace shook her head as if the mere action could erase her thinking. She could not be attracted to this man. And even if her body insisted on betraying her, her mind wouldn't. Her heart wouldn't.

Not again.

She took a deep, shuddering breath and strove for calm.

Control. What she didn't know about Khalis Tannous was whether the reality of a huge billion dollar empire would make him power hungry. Whether the sight of millions of dollars' worth of art made him greedy. Whether he could be trusted.

She'd seen how wealth and power had turned a man into someone she barely recognised. Charming on the outside—and Khalis *was* charming—but also selfish and cruel. Would Khalis be like that? Like her ex-husband?

And why, Grace wondered with a lurch of panic, was she thinking about Khalis and her ex-husband in the same breath? Khalis was her client, no more. Her client with a great deal of expensive art.

Another breath. She needed to think rationally rather than react with emotion, with her memories and fears. This was a different island, a different man. And she was different now, too. Stronger. Harder. Wiser. She had no intention of getting involved with anyone…even if she could.

Deliberately she sat down and pulled a pad of paper towards her. She'd make notes, handle this like any other assignment. She wouldn't think of the way Khalis looked in his swimming trunks, the clean, sculpted lines of his chest and shoulders. She wouldn't remember how he'd made her smile, lightened her heart—something that hardly seemed possible. And she certainly wouldn't wonder if he might end up like his father—or her ex-husband. Corrupted by power, ruined with wealth. It didn't matter. In a few days she would be leaving this wretched island, as well as its owner.

Grace Turner. Khalis stared at the small white card she'd given him. It listed only her qualifications, the name of her company and her phone number. He balanced the card on his knuckles, turning his hand quickly to catch it before he brought it unthinkingly to his lips, almost as if he could catch the scent of her from that little bit of paper.

Grace Turner intrigued him, on many levels. Of course he'd first been struck by her looks; she was an uncommonly beautiful woman. A bit unconventional, perhaps, with her honey-blond hair and chocolate eyes, an unusual and yet beguiling combination. Her lashes were thick and sooty, sweeping down all too often to hide the emotions he thought he saw in her eyes.

And her figure…generous curves and endless legs, all showcased in business attire that was no doubt meant to look professional but managed to be ridiculously alluring. Khalis had never seen a white silk blouse and houndstooth pencil skirt look so sexy. Yet, despite the skyscraper heels, he doubted she intended to look sexy. She was as prickly as a sea urchin, and might as well have had *do not touch* emblazoned on her forehead.

Yet he *did* want to touch her, had wanted it from the moment those gorgeous legs had entered his vision when he'd completed his lap in the pool. He hadn't been able to resist when they'd been in the vault, and her reaction to his taking her hand had surprised, he thought, both of them.

She was certainly a woman of secrets. He sensed her coiled tension, even her fear. Something about this island—about him—made her nervous. Of course, on the most basic level he could hardly blame her. From the outside, Alhaja Island looked like a prison. And he was a stranger, the son of a man whose ruthless exploits had been whispered about if not proved. Even so, he didn't think her fear was directed simply at him, but something greater. Something, Khalis suspected, that had held her in its thrall for a while.

Or was he simply projecting his own emotions onto this mysterious and intriguing woman? For he recognised his own fear. He hated being back on Alhaja, hated the memories that rose to the forefront of his mind like scum on the surface of a pond.

Get used to it, Khalis. This is how it is done.

Don't leave me here, Khalis.

I'll come back...I promise.

Abruptly he rose from his chair, prowled the length of his study with an edgy restlessness. He'd resolutely banished those voices for fifteen years, yet they'd all come rushing back, taunting and tormenting him from the moment he'd stepped on this wretched shore. Despite Eric's tactful suggestion that he set up a base of operations in any number of cities where his father had had offices, Khalis had refused.

He'd run from this island once. He wasn't going to do it again.

And at least the enigmatic and attractive Grace Turner provided a welcome distraction from the agony of his own thoughts.

'Khalis?' He glanced up and saw Eric standing in the doorway. 'Dinner is served.'

'Thank you.' Khalis slid Grace's business card into the inside pocket of the dark grey blazer he'd put on. He felt a pleasurable tingle of anticipation at the thought of seeing the all too fascinating Ms Turner again, and firmly pushed away his dark thoughts once and for all. There was, he'd long ago decided, never any point in looking back.

He'd ordered dinner to be served on a private terrace of the compound's interior courtyard, and the intimate space flickered with torchlight as Khalis strolled up to the table. Grace had not yet arrived and he took the liberty of pouring a glass of wine for each of them. He'd just finished when he heard the click of her heels, felt a prickle of awareness at her nearness. Smiling, he turned.

'Ms Turner.'

'If you insist on my calling you Khalis, then you must call me Grace.'

He inclined his head, more gratified than he should be at her concession. 'Thank you…Grace.'

She stepped into the courtyard, the torchlight casting her into flickering light and wraith-like shadow. She looked magnificent. She'd kept her hair up in its businesslike coil, but had exchanged her work day attire for a simple sheath dress in chocolate-brown silk. On another woman the dress might have looked like a paper sack but on Grace it clung to her curves and shimmered when she moved. He suspected she'd chosen the dress for its supposed modesty, and the fact that she had little idea how stunning she looked only added to her allure. He realised he was staring and reached for one of the glasses on the table. 'Wine?'

A hesitation, her body tensing for a fraction of a second before she held out one slender arm. 'Thank you.'

They sipped the wine in silence for a moment, the night soft all around them. In the distance Khalis heard the whisper of the waves, the wind rustling the palm trees overhead. 'I'd offer a toast, but the occasion doesn't seem quite appropriate.'

'No.' Grace lowered her glass, her slim fingers wrapped tightly around the fragile stem. 'You must realise, Mr Tannous—'

'Khalis.'

She laughed softly, no more than a breath of sound. She did not seem like a woman used to laughing. 'I keep forgetting.'

'I think you want to forget.'

She didn't deny it. 'I told you before, I prefer to keep things professional.'

'It's the twenty-first century, Grace. Calling someone by a first name is hardly inviting untoward intimacies.' Even if such a prospect attracted him all too much.

She lifted her gaze to his, her dark eyes wide and clear with a sudden sobriety. 'In most circles,' she allowed, intriguing him further. 'In any case, what I meant to tell you was that I'm sure you realise most of the art in that vault downstairs has been stolen from various museums around the world.'

'I do realise,' he answered, 'which is why I wished to have it assessed, and assured there are no forgeries.'

'And then?'

He took a sip of wine, giving her a deliberately amused look over the rim of his glass. 'Then I intend to sell it on the black market, of course. And quietly get rid of you.'

Her eyes narrowed, lips compressed. 'If that is a joke, it is a poor one.'

'*If?*' He stared at her, saw her slender body nearly vibrating with tension. 'My God, do you actually think there is any possibility of such a thing? What kind of man do you think I am?'

A faint blush touched her pale cheeks with pink. 'I don't know you, Mr Tannous. All I know is what I've heard of your father—'

'I am nothing like my father.' He hated the implication she was making, the accusation. He'd been trying to prove he was different his whole life, had made every choice deliberately as a way to prove he was not like his father in the smallest degree. The price he'd paid was high, maybe even too high, but he'd paid it and he wouldn't look back. And he wouldn't defend himself to this slip of a woman either. He forced himself to smile. 'Trust me, such a thing is not in the remotest realm of possibility.'

'I didn't think it was,' she answered sharply. 'But it is something, perhaps, your father might have done.'

Something snapped to life inside him, but Khalis could not say what it was. Anger? Regret? *Guilt?* 'My father was not a murderer,' he said levelly, 'as far as I am aware.'

'But he was a thief,' Grace said quietly. 'A thief many times over.'

'And he is dead. He cannot pay for his crimes, alas, but I can set things to rights.'

'Is that what you are doing with Tannous Enterprises?'

Tension tautened through his body. 'Attempting. It is, I fear, a Herculean task.'

'Why did he leave it to you?'

'It is a question I have asked myself many times already,' he said lightly, 'and one for which I have yet to find an answer. My older brother should have inherited, but he died in the crash.'

'And what about the other shareholders?'

'There are very few, and they hold a relatively small percentage of the shares. They're not best pleased, though, that my father left control of the company to me.'

'What do you think they'll do?'

He shrugged. 'What can they do? They're waiting now, to see which way I turn.'

'Whether you'll be like your father.' This time she did not speak with accusation, but something that sounded surprisingly like sympathy.

'I won't.'

'A fortune such as the one contained in that vault has tempted a lesser man, Mr…Khalis.' She spoke softly, almost as if she had some kind of personal experience of such temptation. His name on her lips sent a sudden thrill through him. Perhaps using first names did invite an intimacy…or at least create one.

'I have my own fortune, Grace. But I thank you for the compliment.'

'It wasn't meant to be one,' she said quietly. 'Just an observation, really.' She turned away and he watched her cross to the edge of the private alcove as if looking for exits. The little nook was enclosed by thick foliage on every side but one that led back into the villa. Did she feel trapped?

'You seem a bit tense,' he told her mildly. 'Granted, this island has a similar effect on me, but I wish I could put you at ease in regard to my intentions.'

'Why didn't you simply hand the collection over to the police?'

He gave a short laugh. 'In this part of the world? My father may have been corrupt, but he wasn't alone. Half of the local police force were in his pocket already.'

She nodded, her back still to him, though he saw the tension radiating along her spine, her slender back taut with it. 'Of course,' she murmured.

'Let me be plain about my intentions, Grace. After you've assessed the art—the da Vincis, mainly—and assured me they are not forgeries, I intend to hand the entire collection over to Axis to see it disposed of properly, whether that is the Louvre, the Met, or a poky little museum in Oklahoma. I don't care.'

'There are legal procedures—'

He waved a hand in dismissal. 'I'm sure of it. And I'm sure your company can handle such things and make sure each masterpiece gets back to its proper museum.'

She turned suddenly, looking at him over her shoulder, her eyes wide and dark, her lips parted. It was an incredibly alluring pose, though he doubted she realised it. Or perhaps he'd just been too long without a lover. Either way, Grace Turner fascinated and attracted him more than any woman had in a long time. He wanted to kiss those soft parted lips as much as he wanted to see them smile, and the realisation jarred him. He felt more for this woman than mere physical attraction. 'I told you before,' she said, 'those Leonardos have never been in a museum.'

He pushed away that unwanted realisation with relief. 'Why not?'

'No one has ever been sure they even existed.'

'What do you mean?'

'Did you recognise the subject of the paintings?'

'Something in Greek mythology, I thought.' He racked his brain for a moment. 'Leda and the Swan, wasn't it?'

'Yes. Do you know the story?'

'Vaguely. The Swan was Zeus, wasn't it? And he had his way with Leda.'

'Yes, he raped her. It was a popular subject of paintings during the Renaissance, and depicted quite erotically.' She'd turned to face him and in the flickering torchlight her face looked pale and sorrowful. 'Leonardo da Vinci was known to have done the first painting downstairs, of Leda and the Swan. A romantic depiction, similar in style to others of the period, yet of course by a master.'

'And yet this painting was never in a museum?'

'No, it was last seen at Fontainebleau in 1625. Historians think it was deliberately destroyed. It was definitely known to be damaged, so if it is genuine your father or a previous owner must have had it restored.'

'If it hasn't been seen in four hundred years, how does anyone even know what it looked like?'

'Copies, all based on the first copy done by one of Leonardo's students. You could probably buy a poster of it on the street for ten pounds.'

'That's no poster downstairs.'

'No.' She met his gaze frankly, her eyes wide and a soft,

deep brown. Pansy eyes, Khalis thought, alarmed again at how sentimental he was being. *Feeling.* The guarded sorrow in her eyes aroused a protective instinct in him he hadn't felt in years. Hadn't wanted to feel. Yet one look from Grace and it came rushing back, overwhelming him. He wanted, inexplicably, to take care of this woman. 'In fact,' Grace continued, 'I would have assumed the painting downstairs is a copy, except for the second painting.'

'The second painting,' Khalis repeated. He was having trouble keeping track of the conversation, due to the rush of his own emotions and the effect Grace was having on him. A faint flush now coloured her cheekbones, making her look more beautiful and alluring than ever. He felt his libido stir insistently to life and took a sip of wine to distract himself. What was it about this woman that affected him so much—in so many ways?

'Yes, you see the second painting is one art historians thought Leonardo never completed. It's been no more than a rumour or even a dream.' She shook her head slowly, as if she couldn't believe what she'd seen with her own eyes. 'Leda not with her lover the Swan, but with her children of that tragic union. Helen and Polydeuces, Castor and Clytemnestra.' Abruptly she turned away from him, and with the sudden sweep of those sooty lashes Khalis knew she was hiding some deep and powerful emotion.

'If he never completed it,' he asked after a moment, 'how do art historians even know about its possibility?'

'He did several studies. He was fascinated by the myth of Leda.' Her back was still to him, radiating tension once more. Khalis fought the urge to put his hand on her shoulders, draw her to him, although for a kiss or a hug of comfort he wasn't even sure. He felt a powerful desire to do both. 'He's one of the few artists ever to have thought of painting Leda that way. As a mother, rather than a lover.'

'You seem rather moved by the idea,' he said quietly, and he felt the increase of tension in her lithe body like a jolt of electricity that wired them both.

She drew in a breath that sounded only a little ragged and after a second's pause, turned to him with a cool smile. 'Of course I am. As I told you before, this is a major discovery.'

Khalis said nothing, merely observed her. Her gaze was level, her face carefully expressionless. It was a look, he imagined, she cultivated often. A mask to hide the turbulent emotions seething beneath that placid surface. He recognised it because he had a similar technique himself. Except his mask went deeper than Grace's, soul-deep. He felt nothing while her emotions remained close to the surface, reflected in her eyes, visible in the soft, trembling line of her mouth.

'I didn't mean the discovery,' he said, 'but rather the painting itself. This Leda.'

'I can't help but feel sorry for her, I suppose.' She shrugged, one slender shoulder lifting, and Khalis's gaze was irresistibly drawn to the movement, the shimmery fabric of her dress clinging lovingly to the swell of her breast. She noticed the direction of his gaze and, her eyes narrowed and mouth compressed, pushed past him. 'You mentioned earlier you were starving. Shall we eat?'

'Of course.' He moved to the table and pulled out her chair. Grace hesitated, then walked swiftly towards him and sat down. Khalis inhaled the scent of her perfume or perhaps her shampoo; it smelled sweet and clean, like almonds. He gently pushed her chair in and moved to the other side of the table. Nothing Grace had said or done so far had deterred him or dampened his attraction; in fact, he found the enigmatic mix of strength and vulnerability she showed all the more intriguing—and alluring. And as for the emotions she stirred up in him… Khalis pushed these aside. The events of the last week had left him a little raw, that was all. It should come as no surprise that he was feeling a bit stupidly emotional. It would pass…even as his attraction to Grace Turner became stronger.

Grace laid her napkin in her lap with trembling fingers. She could not believe how unnerved she was. She didn't know if it was being on this wretched island, seeing those amazing paintings, or the proximity to Khalis Tannous. Probably—and unfortunately—all three.

She could not deny this man played havoc with her peace of mind by the way he seemed to sense what she was thinking and feeling. The way his gaze lingered made her achingly aware of her own body, created a response in her she didn't want or like.

Desire. *Need.*

She'd schooled herself not to feel either for so long. How could this one man shatter her defences so quickly and completely? How could she let him? She knew what happened when you let a man close. When you trusted him. Despair. Heartbreak. *Betrayal.*

'So tell me about yourself, Grace Turner,' Khalis said, his voice low and lazy. It slid over her like silk, made her want to luxuriate in its soft, seductive promise. He poured her more wine, which Grace knew she should refuse. The few sips she'd taken had already gone to her head—or was that just the effect Khalis was having on her?

'What do you want to know?' she asked.

'Everything.' He sat back, smiling, the glass of wine cradled between his long brown fingers. Grace could not keep her gaze from wandering over him. Wavy ink-black hair, left just a little long, and those surprising grey-green eyes, the colour of agate. He lifted his brows, clearly waiting, and, startled from her humiliatingly obvious perusal of his attractions, Grace reached for her wine.

'That's rather comprehensive. I told you I did my PhD in—'

'I'm not referring to your professional qualifications.' Grace said nothing. She wanted—had to—keep this professional. 'Where are you from?' he asked mildly, and she let out the breath she hadn't realised she'd been holding.

'Cambridge.'

'And you went to Cambridge for your doctorate?'

'Yes, and undergraduate.'

'You must have done one after the other,' he mused. 'You can't be more than thirty.'

'I'm thirty-two,' Grace told him. 'And, as a matter of fact, yes, I did do one after the other.'

'You know I went to Cambridge?' She inclined her head in acknowledgement; she'd read the file Michel had compiled on him on the plane. 'We almost overlapped. I'm a few years older than you, but it's possible.'

'An amazing coincidence.'

'You don't seem particularly amazed.'

She just shrugged. She had a feeling that if Khalis Tannous had been within fifty miles of her she would have known it. Or maybe she wouldn't have, because then she'd been dazzled by another Cambridge student—her ex-husband. Dazzled and blinded. She felt a sudden cold steal inside her at the thought that Khalis and Loukas might have been acquaintances, or even friends. What if Loukas found out she was here? Even though this trip was business, Grace knew how her ex-husband thought. He'd be suspicious, and he might deny her access to Katerina. *Why* had she let Michel bully her into coming?

'Grace?' She refocused, saw him looking at with obvious concern. 'You've gone deathly white in the space of about six seconds.'

'Sorry.' She fumbled for an excuse. 'I'm a bit tired from the flight, and I haven't eaten since breakfast.'

'Then let me serve you,' Khalis said and, as if on cue, a young woman came in with a platter of food.

Grace watched as Khalis ladled couscous, stewed lamb and a cucumber yogurt salad onto her plate. She told herself it was unlikely Khalis knew Loukas; he'd been living in the States, after all. And, even if he did, he'd surely be discreet about his father's art collection. She was, as usual, being paranoid. Yet she *had* to be paranoid, on her guard always, because access to her daughter was so limited and so precious…and in her ex-husband's complete control.

'*Bon appétit,*' Khalis said, and Grace forced a smile.

'It looks delicious.'

'Really? Because you're looking at your plate as if it's your last meal.'

Grace pressed two fingers to her forehead; she felt the beginnings of one of her headaches. 'A delicious last meal, in any case.' She tried to smile. 'I'm sorry. I'm just tired, really.'

'Would you prefer to eat in your room?'

Grace shook her head, not wanting to admit to such weakness. 'I'm fine,' she said firmly, as if she could make it so. 'And this really does look delicious.' She took a bite of couscous and somehow managed to choke it down. She could feel Khalis's gaze on her, heavy and speculative. Knowing.

'You grew up in Cambridge, you said?' he finally asked, and Grace felt relief that he wasn't going to press.

'Yes, my father was a fellow at Trinity College.'

'Was?'

'He died six years ago.'

'I'm sorry.'

'And I should say the same to you. I'm sorry for the loss of your father and brother.'

'Thank you, although it's hardly necessary.'

Grace paused, her fork in mid-air. 'Even if you were estranged from them, it's surely a loss.'

'I left my family fifteen years ago, Grace. They were dead to me. I did my grieving then.' He spoke neutrally enough, yet underneath that easy affability Grace sensed an icy hardness. There would be no second chances with a man like Khalis.

'Didn't you miss them? At the time?'

'No.' He spoke flatly, the one word discouraging any more questions.

'Do you enjoy living in the States?' she tried instead, keeping her tone light.

'I do.'

'What made you choose to live there?'

'It was far away.'

It seemed no question was innocuous. They ate in silence for a few moments, the only sound the whisper of the waves and wind. When she couldn't see those high walls she could almost appreciate the beauty of this island paradise in the middle of the Mediterranean. Yet she could still *feel* them, knew that the only way out of here was by another person's say-so. At this thought another bolt of pain lanced through her skull and her hand clenched around her fork. Khalis noticed.

'Grace?'

'Did you grow up here?' she asked abruptly. 'Behind these walls?'

He didn't answer for a moment, and his narrowed gaze rested on her thoughtfully. 'Holidays mostly,' he finally said. 'I went to boarding school when I was seven, in England.'

'Seven,' she murmured. 'That must have been hard.'

Khalis just shrugged. 'I suppose I missed my parents, but then I didn't know as much about them as I should have, being only a child.'

'What do you mean?'

'You are most certainly aware that my father was not the most admirable of men.'

'I'm aware.'

'As a child, I did not realise that. And so I missed him.' He said it simply, bluntly, as if it were no more than an obvious fact. Yet Grace was both curious and saddened by his statement. When, she wondered, had Khalis become disillusioned with his father? When he left university? And did learning of a loved one's flaws make you stop loving them? In Khalis's view, it certainly seemed so.

'What about your mother?'

'She died when I was ten,' Khalis told her. 'I don't remember much about her.'

'You don't?' Grace didn't hide her surprise. 'My mother died when I was thirteen, and I remember so much.' The scent of her hand lotion, the softness of her hair, the lullabies she used to sing. She also remembered how dusty and empty their house on Grange Road had seemed after her death, with her father immersed in his books and antiques.

'It was a long time ago,' Khalis said, and although his tone was pleasant enough Grace could still tell the topic of conversation was closed. It almost sounded as if he didn't *want* to remember his mother...or anyone in his past.

She felt an entirely unreasonable flash of curiosity to *know* this man, for she felt with a deep and surprising certainty that he hid secrets. Sorrow. Despite his often light tone, the easy smile, Grace knew there was a darkness and a hardness in him that both repelled and attracted her. She had no business being attracted to any man, much less a man like Khalis. Yet here she was, seeing the sleepy, veiled look in his grey-green eyes, feeling that slow spiral of honeyed desire uncurl in the pit of her belly, even as pain continued to lance her skull. How appropriate. Pain and pleasure. Temptation and torture. They always went together, didn't they?

With effort she returned the conversation to work. 'Tomorrow morning I should like to see the equipment you mentioned,' she told him, keeping her voice brisk. 'The sooner I am able to assess whether the Leonardos are genuine, the better.'

'Do you really doubt it?'

'My job is to doubt it,' Grace told him. 'I need to prove they're real rather than prove they're forgeries.'

'Fascinating,' Khalis murmured. 'A quest for truth. What drew you to such a profession?'

'My father was a professor of ancient history. I grew up around antiques, spent most of my childhood in museums, except for a brief horse-mad phase when all I wanted to do was ride.' She gave him a small smile. 'The Fitzwilliam in Cambridge was practically a second home.'

'Like father like daughter?'

'Sometimes,' Grace said, her gaze locking with his, 'you are your father's child in more than just blood.'

His grey-green gaze felt like a vice on her soul, for she could not look away. It called to something deep within her, something she had suppressed for so long she barely remembered she still possessed it. The longing to be understood, the desire to be known or even revealed. And reflected back in those agate eyes she saw a strange and surprising torment of emotions: sorrow, anger, maybe even despair. Or was she simply looking into a mirror? Her head pounded with the knowledge of what she'd seen and felt, the ache increasing so she longed to close her eyes. Then he broke their gaze, averting his face, his mouth hardening as he looked out at the gardens now cloaked in darkness.

'You must have some dessert,' he finally said, and his voice was as light as ever. 'A Tunisian speciality, almond sesame pastries.' The young woman entered with a plate of pastries as well as a silver tray with a coffee pot and porcelain cups.

Grace took a bite of the sticky sweet pastry, but she could not manage the coffee. Her head ached unbearably now, and she knew if she did not lie down in the dark she would be incapacitated for hours or even days. She'd had these migraines with depressing regularity, ever since her divorce. With an unsteady clatter she returned her coffee cup to its saucer. 'I'm sorry, but I am very tired. I think I'll go to bed.'

Khalis rose from the table, concern darkening his eyes. 'Of course. You look unwell. Do you have a headache?'

Tightly Grace nodded. Spots swam in her vision and she rose from the table carefully, as if she might break. Every movement sent shafts of lightning pain through her skull.

'Come.' Khalis took her by the hand, draping his other arm around her shoulder as he led her from the table.

'I'm sorry,' she murmured, but he brushed aside her apologies.

'You should have told me.'

'It came on suddenly.'

'What do you need?'

'To lie down…in the dark…'

'Of course.'

Then, to Grace's surprise, he pulled her up into his

arms, cradling her easily. 'I apologise for the familiarity, but it is simpler and quicker this way.' Grace said nothing, shock as well as pain rendering her speechless. In her weakened state she didn't have the strength to draw away, nor, she realised, the will. It felt far too good to be held, her cheek pressed against the warm strength of his chest. It had been so very long since she'd been this physically close to someone, since she'd felt taken care of. And even though she knew better than to want it, knew where letting someone take care of you led, she did not even attempt to draw away. Worse, she instinctively, irresistibly nestled closer, her head tucked in the curve of his shoulder. 'You should have told me sooner,' he murmured, brushing a tendril of hair from her cheek, and Grace just closed her eyes. The pain in her head overwhelmed her now, making speech or even thought impossible.

Eventually she heard a door open, felt Khalis lay her gently on a silk duvet. He left, making her feel suddenly, ridiculously bereft, only to return moments later with a cool damp cloth he laid over her forehead. Grace could not keep from groaning in relief.

'Can you manage these?' he said, pressing two tablets in her hand.

She gave the barest of nods. 'What are they?'

'Just paracetamol, I'm afraid. I don't have anything stronger.' He handed her a glass of water and, despite the dagger points of pain thrusting into her skull, she managed to choke the tablets down. She lay back on the bed, utterly spent, in too much pain even to feel humiliated that Khalis was seeing her so weak and vulnerable, and on her very first day.

She felt him slip off her heels, and then he took her feet in his hands and began massaging her soles with his thumbs. Grace lay on the bed in supine surrender as he ministered to her, rubbing his thumbs in deep, slow circles. It felt unbelievably, unbearably good and she felt her headache start to recede, her body relax. She would not have moved even if she possessed the strength to do so.

She must have fallen asleep, for the last thing she remembered until morning was Khalis still rubbing her feet, his touch sure, knowing and so achingly gentle.

CHAPTER FOUR

GRACE woke to sunlight streaming through the crack in the curtains and her head feeling much better. She opened her eyes and stretched, felt a surge of relief mingled with an absurd disappointment that Khalis was gone.

Of course he was gone, she told herself. It was morning. She *wanted* him to be gone. The thought that he might have spent the entire night in her bedroom made her squirm with humiliation. And yet he'd seen enough; she still recalled the gentle way he'd rubbed her feet, how tenderly he'd cared for her. She squirmed some more. She hated feeling weak or vulnerable. Hated the thought of Khalis seeing that and using it to his advantage somehow, even if last night he'd made her feel cherished and cared for.

Forget it, she told herself. *Forget Khalis, forget how he made you feel.* Quickly she rose from the bed, even though it made her head swim a bit. She took a deep breath and staggered to the shower, determined to forget the events of last night and put today on an even and professional keel. She felt better when she'd showered and dressed in work clothes, a pair of slim black trousers and a fitted white T-shirt. She applied the minimum of neutral make-up, pulled her hair back into a ponytail and reached for her attaché case, her professional armour now firmly in place. This was how she needed to be with Khalis, with any man. Professional, strong and completely in control. Not weak or needy. Not wanting.

Khalis's assistant Eric met her at the bottom of the main staircase. He wore a pair of board shorts and a T-shirt with a logo that read 'I work at Silicon Valley. But if I told you more I'd have to kill you'.

Grace thought of her admonition last night. *If that is a joke*... She must have seemed completely ridiculous.

'Ms Turner,' Eric greeted her with an easy smile, 'may I show you to the breakfast room?'

'Thank you.' He led her down a tiled hallway and, curious, she asked, 'Did you meet Mr Tannous in California?'

He turned back to give her a smiling glance. 'How did you know?'

'Oh, I don't know, maybe the hair,' she replied with a small smile. He had light blond hair, bleached by the sun in rather artful streaks. 'Have you known him long?'

'Since he moved out there fifteen years ago. I've been with his gig from the start. He had big ideas and, while I don't have any of those, I'm pretty decent with the admin side.'

'Did you know about his family?'

Eric hesitated for only a second. 'Everyone in California is starting over, more or less,' he said and, although his tone was relaxed, it was also final. He had the same kind of affability Khalis possessed, Grace thought wryly, although rather less of the unyielding hardness she sensed underneath. 'Here you go,' he said, and ushered her into a pleasant room at the back of the building. Khalis was already seated at the table, drinking coffee and reading the newspaper on his tablet computer. He glanced up as she entered, his easy and rather familiar smile making her flush and remember how he'd held her last night. How she'd pressed her cheek against his chest, how he'd rubbed her feet. How much she'd savoured it all. Judging by that smile, he'd probably been able to tell.

'You look like you're feeling better.'

She sat down and poured herself coffee, her gaze firmly on the cup. 'Yes, thank you. I apologise for last night.'

'What is there to be sorry for?'

She added milk. 'I was incapacitated—'

'You were in pain.'

He spoke so quietly and firmly that Grace was startled into looking up, her gaze locking on his green-grey one that was full of far too much understanding. It almost made her want to tell him things. She stirred her coffee and took a sip. 'Still, I am here to perform a set task—'

'And I'm sure you will perform it admirably today. What exactly is on the agenda?'

Relief surged through her as she realised he was going to graciously drop the subject of last night. Today she could talk about. 'First I'll need to catalogue all the works in the vault and check them against the Art Loss Register. Those that appear to have been stolen can be, for the moment, set to one side. Experts from the museums concerned will need to be contacted along with—'

'I'd prefer,' Khalis said, 'not to contact anyone until we know just what we're dealing with.'

Unease crept along her spine with cold fingers. Ridiculous it might be, but she couldn't keep from feeling it. She didn't think Khalis intended to keep the art for himself, but she still didn't trust him. Not on either a professional or personal level. 'And why is that?'

'Because the media storm that will erupt when it is discovered my father had however many stolen paintings in his possession is one I want to control, at least somewhat,' he replied mildly. 'I don't particularly like publicity.'

'Nor do I.'

'And yet,' he said musingly, 'you will certainly be mentioned in any of the articles that will undoubtedly appear.'

'Axis Art Insurers will,' Grace replied swiftly. 'My name will be kept out of it. That has always been our agreement.'

He gazed at her over the rim of his coffee cup. 'You really don't like publicity.'

'No.'

'Then my decision to wait to contact any outside source should meet with your approval.'

'I don't like being managed,' Grace said flatly.

Khalis arched an eyebrow. 'I'd hardly call a request to wait on calling the police being *managed.*'

'It potentially compromises my position.'

'You have a moral objection?'

She bit her lip. She didn't, not really, not if she trusted him to inform the proper legal authority and dispose of the art as necessary. And, logically, she knew she should. She had no real reason to think otherwise, and yet...

And yet she'd once believed a man's assurances. Trusted his promises. Let herself be led into captivity and despair. Every muscle coiled and tightened at the memory. Pain snapped at the edges of her mind, the remnants of her migraine mocking her. *Khalis Tannous is not your ex-husband. Not even close. All you have is a professional relationship.*

'You still don't trust me,' Khalis said quietly. 'Do you? To handle my father's collection properly.'

Grace was not about to admit this wasn't really about the art. It went deeper, darker, and she didn't even understand why. She barely knew this man. She met his gaze as levelly as she could. 'I don't even know you.'

'And yet,' Khalis observed, 'if I intended to keep the paintings or sell them on the black market, contacting your company would be just about the most idiotic thing I could do. Your lack of trust borders on ridiculous, Grace.'

She knew that. She knew his intentions towards the art had to be legitimate. And yet she couldn't keep her frightened instinct from kicking in, from remembering how it felt to be like one of those paintings in that vault, adored and hidden away, for no one else to see. It had been a miserable life for her, just as it was for Leda. And it coloured her response to this man, in shades too dark for her to admit.

And as for what was ridiculous… When he said her name, in really, a completely normal tone of voice…why did it make her insides unfurl, like a seedling seeking sunlight? *That* was absurd. 'It might seem ridiculous to you,' she said stiffly, 'but I've experienced enough to be justified in my lack of trust.'

'Experienced professionally? Or personally?'

'Both,' she said flatly, and began to butter her toast. Khalis was silent for a long moment, but she could still feel his speculation as he sipped his coffee. She'd said too much. Just one word, but it had been too much. Not that it mattered. All it would take was one internet search for Khalis to learn her history, or at least some of it. Not the most painful parts, but still enough to hurt. Perhaps he'd learned it already, although his air of unconcern suggested otherwise.

'So,' he finally said, 'what will you do after you catalogue the paintings and check them against this register?'

'Run preliminary tests on the ones that do not appear to come from any museum. I don't suppose your father kept any files on his artwork?'

'I don't think so.'

'Most paintings of any real value have certificates of

authentication. It's virtually impossible to sell a valuable painting without one.'

'You're saying my father should have these certificates?'

'Of the ones that are not stolen, yes. Obviously the stolen works' certificates would remain with the museums they were taken from. Really, some legal authority should be contacted. Interpol, or the FBI's Art Crimes department—'

'No.' He still spoke evenly enough, but his voice made Grace go cold. It reminded her of Loukas's implacable tone when she'd asked to go to Athens for a shopping trip. One miserable little shopping trip, for things for Katerina. She'd said nothing then, and she said nothing now. Perhaps she hadn't changed as much as she'd hoped. 'I'm not ready to have law enforcement of any kind swarming over this compound and investigating everything.'

'You're hiding something,' she said, the words seeming to scrape her throat.

'My father hid plenty of things,' he corrected. 'And I intend to find out what they all were before I invite the law in.'

'So you can decide which ones to reveal and which ones to keep hiding?'

Ice flashed in his eyes and he leaned forward, his hand encircling her wrist, his movements precise and controlled, yet radiating a leashed and lethal power. 'Let me be very clear. I am not corrupt. I am not a criminal. I do not intend to allow Tannous Enterprises to continue to engage in any illegal activity. But neither do I intend to hand the reins over to a bunch of bureaucratic, bumbling policemen who might be as interested in lining their pockets as my father was. Understood?'

'Let go of my wrist,' she said coldly, and Khalis looked

down as if surprised he was touching her. He hadn't grabbed her, hadn't hurt her at all, yet she felt as if he had.

'I'm sorry.' He released her, then let out a gusty sigh as he raked a hand through his hair. 'I'm sorry if I scared you.' Grace said nothing. She wasn't about to explain that she had been scared, or why. Khalis gave her a thoughtful look from under his lashes, his mouth pursed. 'You've been hurt, haven't you? By a man.'

Shock caused her to freeze, her nerveless fingers almost dropping her coffee cup before she replaced it on its saucer. 'That,' she said, 'is none of your business.'

'You're right. Again, I apologise.' He looked away; the silence in the room felt electric. 'So these preliminary tests. What are they?'

'I need to see what facilities are in the basement. Artwork, especially older artwork, needs to be handled very carefully. A few minutes' exposure to sunlight can cause irreparable damage. But I would expect to analyse the pigments used, as well as use infrared photography to determine what preliminary sketches are underneath the paintings. If I have the right equipment, I can test for the age of the wood of the panels used. This is an especially good way of dating European masters, since they almost always painted on wood.'

'The two in the back room are on wood.'

'Yes.'

'Interesting.' He shook his head slowly. 'Really quite fascinating.'

'I certainly think so.'

He shot her a quick smile and she realised how invigorating it was to have a man actually interested in her work. During their marriage, Loukas had preferred for her never to discuss it, much less practise her chosen profession.

She'd gone along for the sake of marital accord, but it had tried her terribly. Too terribly.

'I'd better let you get to it,' Khalis said, and Grace nodded, pushing away her plate. She'd only eaten half a piece of toast, but she had little appetite.

'Eric will escort you to the basement. Let me know if there is anything you require.' And, with another parting smile, Khalis took his computer and left the room. Grace watched him go, hating that she suddenly felt so lonely.

The rest of the day was spent in the laborious yet ultimately rewarding work of checking all the artworks against the international Art Loss Register. The results were dispiriting. Many of the paintings, as Grace had suspected, were stolen. It made her job of authentication and appraisal easier, yet it saddened her to think of how many paintings had been lost to the public, in some cases for generations.

At noon the young woman who had served her meals earlier brought down a plate of sandwiches and a carafe of coffee. 'Mr Tannous said you needed to eat,' she murmured in hesitant English, and Grace felt a curious mingling of gratitude for his thoughtfulness and disappointment that she wouldn't see him.

Stupid. She hadn't really expected to share another meal with him, had she? Last night had been both an introduction and an aberration. Even so, she could not deny the little sinking feeling she had at the thought of an afternoon working alone. It had never bothered her before; she was certainly used to solitude. It wouldn't bother her now. Frowning, she turned back to her laptop with grim concentration.

Immersed in her work, she wasn't really aware of time passing until she heard a light tap-tap at the door of the lab across from the vault where she'd set up her temporary office. She looked up to see Khalis standing in the doorway. He had changed from his dark trousers and silk shirt of this morning into board shorts and a T-shirt that hugged the lean sculpted muscles of his chest. His hair was a little rumpled.

'You've been at it for eight hours.'

She blinked, surprised even as she felt the muscles in her neck cramp. 'I have?'

'Yes. It's six o'clock in the evening.'

She shook her head, smiling a little, unable to staunch the ripple of pleasure she felt at seeing him. 'I was completely absorbed.'

He smiled back. 'So it would appear. I didn't realise art appraisal was *that* fascinating.'

'I've checked all the works against—'

'No, no talk about art and theft or work. It's time to relax.'

'Relax?' she repeated warily. Both Eric and Khalis seemed big on relaxing, yet she had no intention of letting down her guard, and especially not with this man. Last night's headache episode had been bad enough. She didn't intend to give him another chance to get close, to *affect* her.

'Yes, relax,' Khalis said. 'The sun will set in another hour, and before it does I want to go for a swim.'

'Please, don't let me stop you.'

His mouth quirked in another smile. 'I want you to go with me.'

Her heart seemed to fling itself against her ribs at the thought. 'I don't—'

'Swim? I could teach you. We'll start with the dog paddle.' He mimed a child's paddling stroke and Grace found herself smiling. Again.

'I think I can manage to keep myself afloat, thanks very

much.' Strange, how light he made her feel. How *happy*. It was as dangerous and addictive as the physical response her body had to him. She shook her head. 'I really should get this done—'

Khalis dropped his arms to his sides. 'It's not good to work without taking a break, especially considering the strength of your migraine last night. I let you work through lunch, but you really need to take some time off.'

'Most employers don't insist on their staff taking time off.'

'I'm not most employers. Besides, you're not actually my employee. I'm your client.'

'Still—'

'Anyone with sense knows that people work more effectively when they're rested and relaxed. At least they know that in California.' He held out one hand, his long lean fingers stretching so enticingly towards her. 'Come on.'

She absolutely shouldn't take his hand. *Touch* him. And she shouldn't go for a swim. She shouldn't even *want* to go for a swim, because she didn't want to want anyone ever again. As for love, trust, desire…? Forget it. Forget them all.

And yet… And yet she remained motionless, hesitating, suspended with suppressed longing, because no matter what her brain told her about staying safe, strong and in control, her body and maybe even her heart said differently. They said, *Yes. Please.*

'Do you have a swimming costume?'

Reluctantly she nodded. She had brought one, despite what she'd told Michel.

'Well, then? What's stopping you?'

You. Me. The physical temptation that the very idea of

a swim with Khalis presented. The two of them, in the water and wearing very little.

And then there was the far more alarming emotional temptation...to draw closer to this man, to care about him when she couldn't care about anyone. Never mind what restrictions her ex-husband had placed on her, her heart had far more stringent ones.

'Grace.' He said her name not as a question or a command, but as a statement. As if he knew her. And when he did that Grace felt as though she had no choice, and it both aggravated and amazed her. How could she fight this?

She reached out and took his hand. His fingers closed around hers with both strength and gentleness, and he glanced at her carefully, as if he needed to check she was OK. And, after the way she had yanked her hand away from his last night, he probably did.

Taking a breath, Grace met his questioning gaze—and nodded her assent.

Khalis felt an entirely triumphant thrill as he led her from the basement, up into the sunshine and fresh air. He felt as if he'd won a major victory, not against her, but for her. Something about Grace's hidden vulnerability called out to him, made him want to offer her both protection and pleasure. He'd spent the better part of the day thinking about her, wondering what she was doing, thinking, feeling. Wondering about the man who had hurt her and how soft her lips would be if—*when*—he kissed her.

It had been a long time since he'd been in a relationship, even longer since a woman had aroused these kinds of protective feelings in him. Never before, if he were honest, at least not on a romantic, sexual level. The last woman who he'd been emotionally close to had been his sister. Jamilah.

And look what happened then.

Khalis resolutely pushed the thought away. It was just this island, these memories that were temporarily awakening his emotions.

This woman.

It would pass, Khalis told himself. He'd leave Alhaja and get back to his normal life soon enough. And in the meantime Grace provided a welcome distraction.

Except to think of her as a distraction was to think of her dismissively, as something disposable, and he knew he didn't. Couldn't. Already it had become something more, and he didn't know whether to be alarmed, annoyed or amazed. Perhaps he was all three. But, for right now, all he wanted was a simple swim.

Up in the foyer, she stopped, pulled her hand away from his with firm purpose. 'I need to change.'

'Why don't I meet you at the pool?'

'All right.'

Fifteen minutes later a stiff and self-conscious Grace approached the pool area. He was sitting on the edge of the pool waiting for her, dangling his legs in the water, enjoying the last golden rays of sunshine. He took in her appearance in one swift and silent glance. Her swimming costume was appalling. Well, appalling might be too strong a word. It fitted, at least. But it was black and very modest, with a high neckline and a little skirt that covered her thighs. She looked like a grandmother. A very sexy grandmother, but still. Clearly she meant to hide her attractions. He smiled. Even a ridiculous swimming costume couldn't make Grace Turner unattractive. Her long, slim legs remained on elegant display, and a swimming costume was, after all, a swimming costume. Her generous curves were also on enticing view.

She stiffened under his rather thorough inspection and then tilted her chin in that proud, defensive way he was coming to know so well. He stretched out his hand, which she ignored, instead moving gingerly to the steps that led into the shallow end.

'The water's warm,' he offered.

'Lovely.' She dipped a toe in, then stood on the first step, up to her ankles, looking as if she were being tortured.

'Lovely, you said?' he teased, his voice rich with amusement, and she looked startled before giving him a very small smile.

'I'm sorry. I'm not used to this.'

'And here you told me you could swim.'

Impatiently, she shook her head, gesturing between them with one hand. *'This.'*

And he knew—of course he knew—that she felt it, too. This connection, this energy between them. And, while it alarmed him, he had a feeling it *terrified* her. He saw that, felt it and, without thinking too much about what he was doing—or why—he slipped waist-deep into the water and strode towards her. She watched him approach with wide, wary eyes. He stopped a few feet away and gave her a little splash. She blinked, bewildered.

'What are you doing?'

'Having fun?' Her mouth tightened and she looked quickly away. Intrigued, he asked softly, 'Is there something wrong with that?'

'No,' she said, but she didn't sound convinced. He splashed her again, gently, and to his relief he got a little smile, a sudden flash of fire in her eyes.

'You're asking for it, aren't you?'

Desperately. He waited, watched as she trailed her fingers in the water. She had beautiful fingers, long and slim with elegant rounded nails. His gaze was still fixed on them when she suddenly lifted her hand and hit the water hard with the flat of her palm, sending a wave of water crashing over him, leaving him blinking and spluttering. And laughing, because it was just about the last thing he'd expected.

He sluiced the water from his face and grinned at her. She smiled back, almost tremulously, as if her lips weren't used to it. 'Got you.'

'Yes,' he said, and his voice came out in a husky murmur. 'You did.' Even in that awful swimming costume, she was incredibly, infinitely desirable. And when she smiled he was lost. He felt his fears fall away when he looked at her, any alarm that this was all going too fast and too deep seemed ridiculous. He wanted this. He wanted her. He took a step towards her and she stilled, and then another step so he was close enough to feel her breath feather his face, see the pulse beating in her throat. Then he leaned down and kissed her.

It was the gentlest kind of kiss, his mouth barely brushing over hers. She didn't move away, but she trembled. Her lips parted, but it didn't feel like surrender. It felt like surprise. He reached with one hand to cradle her face, his palm cupping the curve of her cheek, revelling in the satiny softness of her skin. It didn't last more than a few seconds, but it felt endless and yet no time at all. And then it was over.

With a ragged gasp she tore away, stared at him with eyes wide with shock and even anger.

'Grace—'

He didn't get the chance to say any more. As if she had the devil himself on her heels, she scrambled out of the pool, slipping on the wet tiles and landing hard on one knee before lurching upright and running back into the villa.

CHAPTER FIVE

STUPID. Stupid, stupid, stupid idiot—

The litany of self-recrimination echoed remorselessly through her as Grace ran through the villa, pounded up the stairs and then into her room, slamming and locking the door behind her as if Khalis were actually chasing her.

She let out a shuddering breath and then turned from the door, tearing the swimming costume from her body before she went to the en suite bathroom and started the shower.

What had possessed her to go swimming? To splash him? *Flirt?* When he'd moved closer to her in the water she'd known—of course she'd known—what he intended to do. In that moment she'd wanted him to kiss her. And the feel of his lips on hers, his hand on her cheek, had been so unbearably, achingly wonderful—until realisation slammed into her and Katerina's face swam in her vision, reminding her just how much she had to lose.

And not just Katerina, Grace thought with a surge of self-recrimination. What about herself? Her freedom? Her *soul*? Marriage to Loukas had nearly destroyed her. He'd levelled her identity, his words and actions a veritable emotional earthquake, and for years afterwards she'd felt blank, a cipher of a person. Working at Axis had helped restore some of her sense of self, yet she still felt as if she drifted through parts of life, had empty spaces and yawning silences where other people had companionship and joy. And perhaps she always would feel that way, as long as she didn't have her daughter. But she'd at least keep herself, Grace thought fiercely. She'd keep her identity, her independence, her strength. She wouldn't give those away to the first man who kissed her, even if his gentleness nearly undid her.

Grace stepped into the shower and let the hot water rush over her, wash away the memory of Khalis's gentle touch. She felt that endless ache of loneliness deep inside, a well of emptiness she'd convinced herself she'd got used to. Preferred, even. Yet it had only taken one man—one touch—for her to realise just how lonely she really was. She might be strong and safe and independent, but a single kiss had made her achingly aware of the depths of her own unhappiness.

Swallowing hard, she turned off the taps and stepped out of the shower. Work. Work would help. It always did. Quickly she dressed, pulled her damp hair into another serviceable ponytail and then headed downstairs.

Eric had given her a temporary password for the lift's security system and Grace used it, glancing around quickly in search of Khalis. He was nowhere to be found.

Squaring her shoulders, she entered the laboratory that Balkri Tannous had had built to verify the authenticity of the artworks, stolen or otherwise, he acquired on the black market. Grace had been reluctantly impressed by his thoroughness; the laboratory held all the necessary equipment for infrared photography, pigment analysis, dendrochronology and many of the other tests necessary to authenticate a work of art.

She opened her laptop, stared blankly at the catalogue she'd made of the vault's inventory; she'd already checked most of it against the Art Loss Register. It would take another hour or two to finish, yet now she couldn't summon the energy to do it. Instead she slipped off her stool and went back into the vault, past all the canvases in the main room, to the tiny little shrine in the back. She flicked on the lights and sat on the room's one chair; clearly this room had been meant only for Balkri Tannous. She let out a shuddering breath as she stared at the painted wood panels.

The first one, of Leda and the Swan, she'd seen many times before. Not the original, of course, but very good copies. The original, for she didn't really doubt this was the original, had been painted on three wooden panels. The panels had split apart—that had been documented four hundred years ago—but someone had very carefully repaired them. The damaged sections of the painting had been restored, although Grace could still see where the damage had occurred. Still, the painting was incredibly arresting. Leda stood naked and voluptuous, yet with her head bowed in virginal modesty. Her face was turned away as if she were resisting the advances of the sinuous swan, but she had a sensual little half-smile on her face, reminiscent of the Mona Lisa. Did she welcome Zeus's attentions? Had she any idea of the heartbreak that lay ahead of her?

'There you are.'

Grace tensed, even though she wasn't really surprised that Khalis had found her. The overwhelming emotional response she'd felt when he kissed her had receded to a weary resignation that felt far more familiar. Safer, too. 'Do you think she looks happy?' she asked, nodding towards Leda.

Khalis studied the painting. 'I think she's not sure what she feels, or what she wants.'

Grace's gaze remained fixed on Leda's little half-smile, her face turned away from the swan. 'I can't become involved with you, in any way,' she said quietly. 'Not even a kiss.'

Khalis propped one shoulder against the doorway to the little room. 'Can't,' he asked, 'or won't?'

'Both.'

'Why not?'

Another deep breath. 'It's unprofessional to be involved with a client—'

'You didn't sprint from the pool because it was unprofessional.' Khalis cut her off affably enough, although she sensed the steel underneath. 'How's your knee?'

It ached abominably, but Grace had no intention of saying that, or explaining any more. 'There's no point in pressing the matter.'

'You're attracted to me, Grace.'

'It doesn't matter.'

'Do you still not trust me?' he asked quietly. 'Is that it? Are you afraid—of me?'

She let out a little sigh and turned to face him. He looked so achingly beautiful just standing there, wearing faded jeans and a grey T-shirt that hugged the sculpted muscles of his chest. His ink-black hair was rumpled, his eyes narrowed even though he was smiling, a half-smile like Leda's.

'I'm not afraid of you,' she said, and meant it. She might not trust him, but she didn't fear him, either. She simply didn't want to let him have the kind of power opening your body or heart to someone would give. And then, of course, there was Katerina. So many reasons not to get involved.

'What, then?' She just shook her head. 'I know you've been hurt,' he said quietly and she let out a sad little laugh. He was painting his own picture of her, she knew then, a happy little painting like one his god-daughter might make. Too bad he had the wrong paintbox.

'And how do you know that?' she asked.

'It's evident in everything you do and say—'

'No, it isn't.' She rose from the chair, half-inclined to disabuse him of his fanciful notion that she'd been hurt. She *had* been hurt, but not the way he thought. She'd never been an innocent victim, as much as she wished things could be that simple. And she knew, to her own shame and weakness, that she wouldn't say anything. She didn't want him to look at her differently. With judgement rather than compassion, scorn instead of sympathy.

'Why can't you get involved then, Grace?' Khalis asked. 'It was just a kiss, after all.' He'd moved to block the doorway, even though Grace hadn't yet attempted to leave. His face looked harsh now, all hard angles and narrowed eyes, even though his body remained relaxed. A man of contradictions—or was it simply deception? Which was the real man, Grace wondered—the smiling man who'd rubbed her feet so gently, or the angry son who refused to grieve for the family he'd just lost? Or was he both, showing one face to the world and hiding another, just as she was?

It didn't matter. She could not have anything more to do with Khalis Tannous except the barest of professional acquaintances. 'It's complicated, and I don't feel like explaining it to you,' she said shortly. 'But if you've done any digging on the internet, you'll be aware of the details.'

'Is that an invitation?'

She shrugged. 'Just a fact.'

'I'm not some internet stalker,' Khalis told her flatly. 'I'd prefer to hear the truth from you, rather than some gossip website.' She said nothing and he sighed, raking a hand through his hair. Grace nodded towards the exit he was still blocking.

'I should get back to work.'

'It's after seven.'

'Still. If I start running the preliminary tests now, you should have enough information to contact a legal authority in a day or two.'

'Is that what you want?' He gazed at her almost fiercely, and she felt a spasm of longing to walk into his arms, to tell him everything. To feel safe and desired all at once.

Ridiculous. *Dangerous.* To do such a thing would be to open herself up to all kinds of shame and pain, and it would certainly put an end to feeling safe or desired.

'Of course it is,' she said and made to walk past him. He didn't move, so she had to squeeze past in the narrow doorway, her breasts brushing his chest, every point of contact seeming to sizzle and snap her nerve endings to life. She looked up at him, which was a mistake. His eyes blazed need and for an endless charged moment she thought he would kiss her again. He'd grab her and take her right there, with Leda watching with her half-smile. She wouldn't resist, not in that moment. She wouldn't be able to. But instead he stepped back and as she moved past he let out a shuddering breath. She kept walking.

Half an hour later he sent a dinner tray down to the lab. He'd included a snowy-white linen napkin, sterling silver cutlery, and even a carafe of wine and a crystal wine glass. His thoughtfulness made her ache. Did he realise how he was taking apart her defences with these little gestures? Could he possibly know how much they hurt, because they made her afraid and needy all at once?

She picked at the meal, alone in the sterile, windowless lab, feeling lonelier than ever and hating that she did.

Then she determinedly pushed the tray away and turned back to her work.

She didn't see him all the next day, although she felt his presence. At breakfast he'd left a newspaper by her plate, already turned to the Arts section. He'd even written a funny little comment next to one of the editorials, making her smile. She pushed the paper away and drank her coffee and ate her toast alone before heading back downstairs.

Work kept her from thinking too much about him, although he remained on the fringes of her mind, haunting her thoughts like a gentle ghost. She'd had Eric help her move the panels into the lab, and she started running a basic dendrochronology test on the wood. At noon the young woman—her name, Grace had learned, was Shayma—brought her sandwiches and coffee. The tray also held a narrow vase with a single calla lily. After Shayma had left Grace reached for the lily and brushed the fragrant petals against her lips. She closed her eyes, remembering how Loukas had sent her roses. She'd been so touched at the time, grieving her father's death, needing someone's attention and love. Only later did she wonder if the flowers had been a genuine expression of his affection, or just a rote seduction. Did it even matter when things had broken down, or what had been real? She'd learned her lesson. She'd learned it the hard way, which was why this had to stop.

She shoved the tray away and turned back to her work. She worked the rest of the day, through dinner, and went directly up to her room. Both exhausted and restless, she fell into an uneasy sleep.

The next day followed the same pattern. She analysed the pigments used in both the Leonardos, and ate from trays brought down by Shayma. And thought about Khalis.

She could feel his presence in every thoughtful touch, from the different flowers on her tray to the newspaper left on the breakfast table, to the subtle changes in the lab: better lighting, a more comfortable chair. How did he even know? She didn't see him at all, though, and she realised she missed him.

An emotion, she knew, she didn't want and couldn't afford to feel. Over the last four years loneliness was a price she'd always been willing to pay for her freedom. Yet in just the space of a few days Khalis had opened up a sweet yearning inside her, a longing for a closeness she'd denied herself and half-forgotten. A longing that terrified her on so many levels.

That night she left the lab craving fresh air, and slipped out of the doors in the back of the entrance hall that led to the interior courtyard of the villa. She stopped by the pool, now still and empty, and realised by the flash of disappointment she felt that she'd been hoping to see him there. Amazing, how deceptive her own heart could be. She'd convinced herself she simply wanted some air but, really, she wanted Khalis.

She pressed her hands to her temples, as if she could will the want away. *Think what you have to lose. Your daughter. The precious moments you have with her. One Saturday a month. Just twelve days a year.*

She started walking down one of the twisting garden paths as fast as she could, as if she could outrun her thoughts. But they chased her, relentless in their power. *Let a man close and not only will you lose your daughter, you'll lose yourself. Khalis can't be that different. And, even if he is...you aren't.*

Yet right now she wanted to be different. She craved the possibility of a loving, generous, equal relationship.

Impossible. Even if it existed, she couldn't have it. She

couldn't risk it, and yet, for the sake of one man, one unbearably kind and gentle man, she was tempted to try. To throw it all away—and for what? A kiss? An affair? She could not believe she could be so weak…again.

Suddenly a pair of strong hands clamped around her shoulders and she let out a shocked yelp.

'It's just me.' Khalis loomed in front of her, his smile gleaming in the moonlight. She could feel the heat radiating from his lithe body.

'You startled me.'

'So I see.' He released her and stepped back. 'I was out here walking as well, and you almost crashed into me.'

'I'm sorry.'

'It's OK.'

They stood there, a foot or so separating them, yet, considering the nature of her recent thoughts, it felt like an endless chasm. She wanted to walk into his arms and run away both at the same time. She was, Grace thought, an emotional schizophrenic. The sooner she got off this island the better.

'Do you want to walk with me?' Khalis asked and, after a charged pause, she nodded. *Compromise.* There was not room on the narrow little paths to walk side by side, so Khalis let her go first, wending her way among the fragrant foliage, the silver swathe the moon cut through the gardens their only guide.

'Did you play out here?' Grace asked. 'When you were a child?'

Khalis shrugged. 'Sometimes.'

'With your brother?'

'Not really. With my…' A second's pause. 'With my sister.'

'I didn't realise you had a sister.'

'She died.'

'Oh!' Grace turned around. Even in the darkness she saw how hooded his expression seemed. 'So your whole family has died,' she said quietly. 'I'm sorry.'

'So has yours.'

'Yes…' She felt a shudder run through her. 'But it must be harder for you, to lose siblings—'

'I do miss my sister,' Khalis said, the words seeming to be drawn reluctantly from him, although he spoke with a quiet evenness. 'I never had a chance to say goodbye to her.'

'How did she die?'

'A boating accident, right off the coast here. She was nineteen.' He sighed, digging his hands into his pockets. 'She was about to be married. My father had arranged it, but she didn't like the chosen groom.'

Grace frowned, connecting the pieces, threaded together by the darkness of Khalis's tone. 'Do you think it…it wasn't an accident?'

He didn't answer for a long moment. 'I don't know. I hate to think that, but she was determined in her own way, and it would have been a way to escape the marriage.'

'A terrible way.'

'Sometimes life is terrible,' Khalis said, and his voice was bleak. 'Sometimes there are only terrible choices.'

'Yes,' Grace said quietly. 'I think that's true.'

He gave her a wryly sorrowful smile, his teeth gleaming in the darkness. 'I never speak of my sister. Not to anyone. What is it about you, Grace, that makes me say things I wouldn't say to another soul? And *want* to say them?'

She shook her head, her heart thudding treacherously. 'I don't know.'

'Do you feel it?' he asked in a low voice, and in the soft darkness of the garden she couldn't deny or pretend.

'Yes,' she said, the word no more than a thread of sound.

'It scares you.'

Of course it does. She took a deep breath. 'I told you before, I can't—'

'Don't give me that,' Khalis said almost roughly. 'You think this is easy for me and hard for you?'

'No—' Yet she realised she had thought that. He seemed so relaxed and assured, so comfortable with what stretched and strengthened between them, and she was the only one quaking with nerves and memories and fear. She let out a wobbly laugh. 'Maybe it's just the island.'

'The island?'

She gestured to the dense fragrant foliage around them. 'It's like a place and time apart, separate from reality. We can say what we want here. Feel what we want.'

'Except,' Khalis said quietly, 'I don't think you know what you want to feel.'

She felt a sudden spark of anger. 'Don't patronise me.'

'Am I wrong?'

She swallowed and looked away. 'I already explained to you—'

'You didn't explain anything,' Khalis said, cutting her off. He sighed, stepping towards her, his hand resting on her shoulder. 'Life hasn't been very fair to you, has it, Grace?'

She tensed under his touch, as well as his assumption. 'Life isn't very fair,' she said in a low voice.

'No,' Khalis agreed. His hand was warm and heavy on her shoulder, a comforting weight she longed to lean into. 'Life isn't very fair at all. I think we've both learned that the hard way.'

Her whole body tensed, fighting the desire to lean into him. It was like trying to resist a magnetic force. 'Maybe,' she said, the word half-strangled.

'And here we are,' he mused softly, 'two people completely alone in this world.'

Her throat tightened with emotion. This man made her feel so much. 'I feel alone,' she whispered, the words drawn from her painfully. She almost choked on them. 'I feel alone all the time.'

His hand still rested on one shoulder, and he laid his other hand on her shoulder and drew her gently to him. 'I know you do,' he said quietly. 'So do I.' She rested in the circle of his arms for a moment, savouring the closeness as she breathed in the woodsy scent of his aftershave, felt the comforting heat of his body. It felt so good, so safe, and it would be so easy to stay here, or even to tilt her head up for him to kiss her. So easy, and so dangerous.

Think what you have to lose.

Resolutely she turned away from him, jerking away from his grasp, not wanting him to see the storm of unwilling need she knew would be apparent on her face. She plunged down the twisting path, only to stop abruptly when it ended against a stone wall. The wall that surrounded the villa, the moon illuminating the evil shards of broken glass on its top, reminding her that she was a prisoner. Always a prisoner.

In a sudden burst of fury, Grace slapped her hands against the stone, her palms stinging, as if she could topple it over. 'I hate walls,' she cried in frustration, knowing it was a ridiculous thing to say, to *think*, yet feeling it with every breath and bone.

'Then let's leave them behind,' Khalis said and reached for her hand. Too surprised to resist, she let him lead her away from the wall and down another dark path.

Khalis kept hold of her hand as he guided her down several paths and then finally to a door. The high, forbidding wall had a door, and Khalis possessed the key. Grace watched as he activated the security system, first with his fingerprint and then a number code, before swinging the door open and leading her out to freedom.

The air felt cooler, fresher and more pure without the walls. Khalis led her away from the compound and down a rocky little path towards the shore.

He still held her hand, his fingers wrapped warm and sure around hers as he guided her down the path to the silky sweep of sand. She heard the roar of the waves crashing onto the shore and saw the beach nestled in a rocky cove, now washed in silver.

'This feels better,' she said, as if she'd just had a little dizzy spell.

'Why do you hate walls so much?'

She tugged her hand out of his. 'Who likes them?'

'Nobody really, I suppose, but it seems personal to you.'

Grace kept her gaze on the silvered sea. 'It is. I used to live on an island like this. Private, remote, with high walls. I didn't like it.'

'Couldn't you leave?'

'Not easily.'

She could feel him staring at her, trying to figure her out, even though her back was to him. 'Are you saying,' he asked finally, 'you were some kind of prisoner?'

She sighed. 'Not really. Not literally. But other things can imprison you besides walls.' She turned so she was half-facing him. 'Hopes. Fears.' She paused, her gaze sliding to and then locking with his. 'Mistakes. Memories.'

She felt tension snake through him, even though he kept his voice light. 'That sounds like psychobabble.'

'It probably is,' she admitted with a shrug. 'But can you really deny this island has an effect on you?'

Khalis didn't answer for a moment. 'No,' he said finally, 'I can't.'

Neither of them spoke for a moment, the truth of what he'd said seeming to reverberate through them. 'What will you do with this place?' Grace asked eventually. 'Will you live here?'

He gave a harsh laugh. 'After what you just observed? No, never. Once I've finished going through my father's assets, I'll sell it.'

'Will you manage Tannous Enterprises from the States, then?'

'I don't intend to manage Tannous Enterprises at all. I'm going to dismantle it and sell it off piece by piece, so no one has that kind of power again.'

'Sell it?' Even in the moonlit darkness she could make out the hard set of his jaw, the flintiness in his eyes. 'I thought you were going to turn it around. Redeem it.'

He looked away from her, out to the sea. 'Some things can't be redeemed.'

'Do you really think so?' She felt a sudden sorrowful twist of disappointment inside her. 'I like to think they can. I like to think any…mistake can be forgiven, if not rectified.'

'My father is not alive for me to forgive him,' Khalis said flatly. 'If I even wanted to.'

'You don't?'

'Why should I? Do you know what kind of man my father was?'

'Sort of, but—'

'Shh.' Smiling now, Khalis drew her to him and pressed one finger to her lips. His touch was soft and yet electric, the press of his skin against her lips making the bottom of her stomach seem to drop right out. 'I didn't bring you to this moonlit cove to talk about my father.'

'I could tell you about what I've discovered about the panels—' Grace began. Her heart beat hard in her chest for she could not mistake the look of intent in Khalis's eyes. Or the answering pulse of longing she felt in herself.

He laughed softly. 'I didn't bring you here for that, either.'

Her heart thudded harder. 'Why, then?'

'To have you kiss me.'

Shock made her mouth drop right open and he traced the curve of her parted lips with the tip of his finger. A soft sigh escaped her before she could suppress it. 'Kiss you—'

'The reaction when I kissed you was not quite what I was hoping for,' Khalis explained, a hint of humour in his voice although his gaze blazed into hers. 'So I thought perhaps we'd try it the other way.'

His finger still rested on her mouth, making her dizzy. 'How do you know I even want to kiss you?' she challenged.

'Do you?'

How could she lie? His gaze was hungry and open; he hid nothing. And she hid so much. From him, and even from herself. For even if she didn't want to want him, she knew she did. And she wouldn't hide it. 'Yes,' she whispered, and Khalis waited.

Grace took a shuddering breath. Just one kiss. One kiss no one would ever know about. And then she'd walk away, go back to being safe and strong and independent. Slowly she reached out and touched his cheek, his own hand falling away from her mouth. She took a step towards him so her breasts brushed his chest. He gazed down at her, still, steady. Trustworthy.

Her palm cradled his cheek, the tips of her fingers brushing the softness of his hair. She leaned closer, so her body pressed fully against his and she could feel the hard thrust of his arousal. And then she kissed him.

CHAPTER SIX

HER lips barely brushed his, but Khalis held himself still, and Grace knew he was purposely letting her control the kiss. She closed her eyes, luxuriating in the feel and taste of him. He tasted like mint and whisky, a sensual combination. His lips were soft and yet his yielding touch was firm, so that even though she was in charge she knew it was only because he allowed it. And somehow that made her feel safe rather than threatened or repressed.

Gently she touched her tongue to his lips, exploring the seam of his mouth, the caress a question. She felt a shudder go through him but he didn't move. She pulled away, blinking up at him with a new shyness. She saw his eyes were closed, his body rigid. He looked almost as if he were in pain, but surely he couldn't be...unless it was costing him to remain so still.

'A kiss involves a bit of give and take, you know,' she told him.

He opened his eyes, giving her a wry smile. 'I didn't want to scare you off.'

'I don't scare quite that easily.' At least she hoped she didn't.

'No?' His arms came around her, gently, slowly, giving her time to pull away. She didn't. She'd allow herself this one moment, that was all. In a minute she'd step away.

'Good,' Khalis murmured, and Grace slid her hands up along the hard wall of his chest, lacing her fingers around his neck as she pulled his mouth down towards her. And then she kissed him again, deeply this time, a plunging sensation in her stomach as he responded in kind, their tongues tangling in a blaze of exquisite sensation. When had she last kissed like this? Felt like this?

You know when.

A shudder ran through her, a shudder of both longing and loss. It felt so wonderful and it had been so long, and yet just the memory of a man holding her made the memories rise up, the shame rushing through her in a hot, fast river, along with the desire and the hope. She closed her eyes and kissed Khalis more deeply, pressing herself against him, wanting desperately to banish the memories that taunted her even now.

You kissed a man like this. You wanted a man like this. And it cost you your daughter.

She felt Khalis's hands span her waist, then slide under her T-shirt. The warmth of his palm against her skin made her shudder again and he stilled, waiting. He was so careful, so *caring*, yet she could not halt the relentless encroaching of her memories and that cold hard logic that swamped even her desire, and she knew he felt it, too.

'Grace…?'

She pulled away from him, her head bowed, her hair falling in front of her face. 'I'm sorry.'

'No need to be sorry.' He took her chin in his hand so he could study her face. See her blush. 'We don't need to rush this, do we?'

Yes, she wanted to say, *we do. Because this is all we have.*

'I shouldn't have kissed you.'

'It's a little late for regrets,' he said wryly and Grace jerked her chin from his hand.

'I know that.'

'Why shouldn't you have kissed me, Grace?'

'Because—' Her breath came out in a rush. *Because I'm scared. Of so many things. Of losing myself in you, and losing my daughter as well.* How could she explain all that? She couldn't, didn't want to, because to explain was to open herself up to all kinds of vulnerability and pain. She just shook her head.

Khalis let out a slow breath, the sound of controlled impatience. 'Are you married or something?'

She forced herself to meet his gaze levelly. 'No. But I was.'

He stilled, his eyes narrowing. 'You're divorced?'

'Yes.'

'I still don't understand.'

'It's…complicated.'

'That much I could guess.'

She turned away, wrapping her arms around herself. Now the wind felt cold. 'I just can't be involved with you,' she said quietly. 'My marriage wasn't… It wasn't happy. And I'm not…' She let out a little weary sigh. 'I can't…' She stopped again, her throat too tight for any more words.

'What,' he asked, 'would it take for you to trust me?'

Grace turned back to him, and she saw a man who had only been gentle and patient and kind. 'I don't know,' she whispered. 'But it doesn't matter, Khalis. I wish it did matter, in a way. But, even if I wanted to, I couldn't be in a relationship with you.' Belatedly she realised he'd never actually said that word. *Relationship.* It implied not just intimacy, but commitment. 'Or anything,' she added hurriedly. 'There can't be anything between us.' And, before he could answer, she walked quickly down the beach, back towards the door and that high, high wall.

That night she slept terribly. Memories came in fragments, as dreams, bizarre and yet making too much sense. Khalis kissing her. Her kissing Khalis. The sweet yearning of it, suddenly obliterated by the shame and guilt as she stared into Loukas's face so taut with anger, his lips compressed into an accusing line.

How could you do this to me, Grace? How could you betray me so?

With a cry she sat up in bed, the memory roiling through her mind, racking her body with shudders. Knowing she would not be able to get back to sleep, she rose from the bed and pulled on a pair of jeans and a light cotton jumper. She piled her hair up with a clip and slipped out of her room, along the cool, dark corridors and downstairs.

The basement felt eerily still in the middle of the night, even though Grace knew it should make no difference. The place had no windows. She switched on the lights and gazed down at the panels laid out on a stainless steel table.

She'd spent most of her time so far authenticating the first painting of Leda and the Swan, but now she let her gaze turn to the second painting, the one that caused a fresh shaft of pain to lance through her. Leda and her children.

Over the centuries there had been speculation about this painting; Leonardo had done several studies, a few sketches of Leda sitting, her face downcast, her children by her side. Yet the reality of the actual painting was far more powerful than any sketch. Unlike the other painting, in this one Leda was seated and clothed, the voluptuous temptress hidden or perhaps forgotten. Two children, Castor and Polydeuces, stood behind her, sturdy toddlers, their hands on her shoulders as if they were anchoring them-selves, or perhaps protecting their mother. Clytemnestra and Helen were rotund babies, lolling in Leda's lap, their angelic faces upturned towards their mother.

And Leda... What was the expression on her face? Was it sorrow, or wistfulness, or even a wary joy? Was there knowledge in those lowered eyes, knowledge of the terri-ble things to come? Helen would start a war. Castor would die in it. And Clytemnestra would lose a daughter.

Abruptly Grace turned away from the painting. If she worked for a few hours, she could present Khalis with a file of her findings tomorrow, enough for him to go on with, and for her to leave Alhaja. Leave Khalis. And they could both get on with their lives.

Khalis watched as a wan and fragile-looking Grace entered the breakfast room the next morning. She looked as if she'd barely slept, although her pale face was composed and as lovely as ever. She was dressed in a slim-fitting black skirt and white silk blouse and carried a file, and Khalis knew exactly what she was about. After last night's frustrating and half-finished kiss, he'd expected something like this. He sat back in his chair and sipped his coffee, waiting for her to begin.

'I've completed most of the preliminary tests on the Leonardos.'

'You have?'

She placed the file on the table, her lips pressed together in determination. 'Yes. The analyses of the pigments and the wood panels are consistent with the time period that he would have completed these paintings. There are also several—'

'Grace.'

She stopped, startled, and Khalis smiled at her. 'You don't need to give me a lecture. I'll read the file.'

Her lips thinned even more. 'All right, then.'

Khalis took a sip of his coffee. 'So you feel you've finished?'

'I've done all that I can do on my own. You really need to call a legal authority to—'

'Yes, I'll take care of that.'

She stopped, her eyes narrowing, and Khalis felt a sliver of hurt needle his soul. Did she *still* not trust him about the damn art? Then slowly, resolutely, she nodded. Acceptance, and he felt a blaze of gratified triumph.

'Very well.' She straightened, pressed her hands down the sides of her skirt. 'Then my work here is done. If you could arrange—'

'Done? Good.' Khalis smiled, saw the flash of hurt in her chocolate eyes that was quickly veiled. Suppressed, but he'd seen it and it gave fire to his purpose. No matter what she'd said last night, no matter how her ex-husband had hurt her so badly she trembled at the thought of a kiss, she still wanted to be with him. 'Then you can take the day off.'

'What…what do you mean?'

'A day of leisure, to enjoy yourself. With me.'

'I don't—'

'Your work was expected to take a week. It's been three days. I think you can take a day off.'

'I told you before—'

'One day. That's all. Surely you can allow yourself that?'

She hesitated, and he saw the longing in her eyes. What, he wondered yet again, kept her from enjoying herself? From *living*? 'You want to.' He leaned forward, not bothering to hide the need he was sure she could see in his eyes. The need he was sure she felt, too. '*I* want to. Please, Grace.'

Still she hesitated. Khalis waited. 'All right,' she said at last. She offered him a rather tentative smile. 'All right.'

Khalis couldn't keep himself from grinning. 'Wonderful. You'd better change into something a bit more serviceable, and I'll meet you in the foyer in five minutes.'

'That's rather quick.'

'I want to take advantage of every moment with you.'

A flush tinted her cheeks rose-pink and she turned away. 'One day,' she murmured, and he couldn't tell if she was warning him—or herself.

Grace hadn't brought too many serviceable clothes with her, at least not the kind she thought Khalis had in mind. While working she dressed with discreet professionalism, clothes that were flattering without being obvious. After a few moments' consideration she chose the slim black trousers and white fitted T-shirt she'd worn earlier in the week, and threw a cardigan in charcoal-grey cashmere over her shoulders, in case the breeze from the sea was strong.

Where could he be taking her? Alhaja Island hadn't looked that large from the air. Besides the enclosed compound, there were only a few stretches of beach and a tangle of trees. Yet Grace knew it didn't even matter where he might be taking her, because she simply wanted to be with him—for one day. One day that posed no risk to her heart or her time with Katerina. One day out of time and reality, a memory she would carry with her in all the lonely days and nights ahead.

Khalis was already waiting in the foyer when she came down the stairs, wearing jeans and a white button-down shirt, open at the throat, so Grace's gaze was inexorably drawn to that column of golden-brown skin, the pulse beating strongly. She jerked her gaze upwards and gave him a tentative smile.

'Where are we going?'

'Just to the beach,' he said, but there was a glint in his eye that told her he had something planned. Grace followed him outside to an open-topped Jeep waiting in the drive. She climbed in and fastened her seat belt as Khalis drove through the forbidding-looking gates and then out along a rutted dirt road that looked to circumnavigate the island.

Grace pushed her hair from her face and shaded her eyes as she glanced at the rocky outcrops and the stretch of golden beach, the sea jewel-bright and winking under the sun in every direction. 'This island's not very big, is it?'

'Two miles long and half a mile wide. Not large at all.'

'Did you ever feel…trapped? Living here?'

Khalis slid her a speculative glance and Grace pretended not to notice. 'Yes,' he answered after a moment, his hands tightening reflexively on the steering wheel, 'but not because of the island's size.'

'Why, then?'

His mouth curved grimly. 'Because of the island's inhabitants.'

'Your father?'

'Mainly. My brother and I didn't get along very well, either.'

'Why not?'

He shrugged. 'Ammar was my father's heir, and my father poured everything into him. He was tough with him, too tough, and I suppose Ammar needed to take it out on someone.'

'He was a bully? Your brother?'

Khalis just shrugged again. 'Boarding school was a bit of a relief.'

'What about your sister?'

He didn't answer for a moment, and Grace felt the tension in his body. 'I missed her,' he finally said. 'I'm sure she felt more trapped here than I did. My father didn't believe in educating daughters. He employed a useless governess for a while, but Jamilah never had the opportunities Ammar and I did. Opportunities she would have had if—' He stopped suddenly, shaking his head. His expression, Grace saw, had become shuttered. Closed. 'Old memories,' he said finally. 'Pointless.'

'Do you think,' she asked after a moment, 'the helicopter crash was an accident?'

'It's not outside the realm of possibility that one of his enemies—or even his allies—tinkered with the engine. I don't know what they would have hoped to gain. Perhaps it was an act of revenge—my father did business with the dregs of every society. People like that tend not to die in their beds.'

Grace felt a chill of trepidation at how indifferent Khalis sounded, as if the way his father and brother had died was a matter of little concern. His attitude towards his family was so different from the affable man she'd come to know and even to trust. Again she glimpsed a core of hard, unyielding iron underneath all that easygoing friendliness. 'You sound rather heartless,' she told him quietly.

'*I* sound heartless?' Khalis gave a short laugh. 'Good thing you never met my father.'

Grace knew she could not explain to Khalis why his opinion of his father disquieted her so much. She had heard rumours of Balkri Tannous, the bribes he took, the kind of shady business he conducted. Why was she, in her own twisted way, trying to defend him?

Because you still feel guilty. In need of forgiveness. Just like him.

'How did you find out?' she asked and Khalis did not pretend to misunderstand.

'I was sixteen,' he said quietly. 'Home from school for the summer holidays. I went looking for my father, to tell him I'd won the mathematics prize that year.' He lapsed into a silence and Grace knew he was remembering, saw the pain of that memory in the tautness of his face. 'I found him in his study. He was on the telephone, and he waved for me to sit down. I couldn't help but overhear him—not that he was trying to hide it. At first I didn't understand. He said something about money, and asking for more, and I thought he was just talking about business. Then he said, "You know what to do if he resists. Make sure he feels it this time." It sounded like something a school bully would say. I'd certainly heard such talk at school. But coming from my father—I couldn't credit it. So much so that when he got off the telephone I asked him about it, almost as if it were a joke. "Papa," I said, "it almost sounded like you were ordering someone to be beaten up!" My father gave me one hard look and then he said, "I was."'

Khalis said nothing more. He'd pulled the Jeep onto a flat stretch of beach and killed the engine, so the only sound was the crash of waves onto the shore and the distant raucous cry of gulls. 'And what then?' Grace asked, for she knew there was more.

He lifted one shoulder in something close to a shrug. 'I was shocked, of course. I don't remember what I said—something stupid about it being wrong. My father came over to me and slapped my face. Hard.' With a small smile he gestured to a tiny white scar on the corner of his mouth. 'His ring.'

'That's terrible,' Grace said quietly.

'Oh, it's not that terrible. I was sixteen, after all, almost a man. And he didn't hit me again. But it was shocking to me because he'd never hit me before. I'd adored him, and he loved to be adored. Ammar had it much worse. My father didn't pay much attention to me, although I always wanted him to. Until that day, when I realised just what kind of man he was.'

'But you didn't leave until you were twenty-one.'

Khalis's mouth tightened before he gave a hard smile. 'No. I made justifications for his activities, you see. Excuses. It was only the one time. The person he was dealing with was difficult or corrupt. So many absurd excuses because I didn't have the courage to just leave.'

'You were young,' Grace said softly. 'And that's easy to do.'

'For a while, perhaps, but then it's just wilful blindness. Even when I didn't want to, I started noticing things. The way the servants shrank from him, the telephone conversations he had. And then I started doing a bit of digging—I went through his desk once when he was away on business. He hadn't even locked his office—too arrogant to think his family would nose about. I probably saw enough in that one afternoon to put him in prison.' He shook his head. 'He helped rig an election in an island country that was desperately poor. My father lined his pockets and the people got poorer.'

'What did you do then?'

'Nothing.' Khalis practically spat the word. 'I was nineteen, about to start Cambridge, and I knew I couldn't manage on my own. So I just put it all back and tried to forget about it—for a little while at least. But I couldn't forget. I'll never forget.' Khalis shook his head, his eyes narrowed against the harsh glare of the sun, or perhaps just in memory.

Grace swallowed. 'And so you left.'

'Finally.' The one word was harsh with self-recrimination. 'I took his money to go to university first. I didn't work up the courage to leave until I knew I could make a go of it on my own.' His mouth twisted in condemnation of his own actions. 'So I wasn't really much better than he was.'

'That's rather harsh,' Grace protested. 'You weren't responsible for your father's actions.'

'No. But doing nothing can be as damaging as the action itself.'

'You were young—'

'Not that young.' He turned to her with a quick smile, his expression clearing although Grace still saw the storm clouds lurking in the depths of his agate eyes. 'You're very forgiving, much more forgiving than I am.' Grace looked away. Yes, she tried to be forgiving because she knew how easy it was to fall. The only person she couldn't forgive was herself. 'We've talked about this enough,' Khalis said. 'I didn't intend to spend the day with you raking up bitter memories. What is done, is done.'

'Is it?' Grace asked, her voice hoarse as she stared out to sea. 'Or does it just go on and on?'

Khalis gazed at her for a moment. 'It is done,' he said quietly. 'Whatever it is, Grace, it is done.'

She knew he didn't know what he was talking about, what secrets she still hid, and yet even so she wanted to believe him. She wanted to believe that things could really be finished, sins truly forgiven. His father's…and hers. She wanted to believe in a second chance even if she never got one. Silently she took his hand and let him lead her out of the Jeep.

They walked down the beach, Khalis's hand still loosely linked with her own, until they came to a sheltered spot, the rocks providing protection from the relentless wind.

Grace stopped in surprise at the sight of two gorgeous horses, a bay mare and a chestnut stallion, saddled and waiting, a groom holding their reins.

'What—?'

'I thought you might like to go riding.'

She shot him a sideways glance. 'How do you even know if I ride?'

'You mentioned a horse-mad phase,' Khalis said with a smile. 'That first night.'

'So I did.' She'd forgotten. She'd almost forgotten how to ride. She stared at the horses, reached out to stroke the bay's satiny coat. 'And I suppose you've been riding since the day you were born?'

'Only since I was two. But it's been a while.'

'For me, too.'

'We can take it slowly.'

Were they talking about riding, Grace wondered, or something else? It didn't really matter. She was touched Khalis had thought of this, had remembered her offhand comment. And she wanted to ride. With a smiling nod she let the groom help her to mount. She was glad Khalis had told her to wear serviceable clothing.

Khalis mounted his own horse and smiled at Grace. 'Ready?'

She nodded again, surprised and gratified by how much she enjoyed the feel of riding again, the wind at her back, the sun shining down. She nudged the horse into a canter and Khalis followed suit, the horses happy to trot down the length of the beach.

The breeze ruffled her hair and gulls cried raucously overhead. Grace felt a grin bloom all over her face. She'd forgotten how free she felt when she rode, how everything seemed to shrink to a point of a pin, the cares and fears and even the memories. Nothing mattered but this moment. Without even realising she was doing so, she urged her mount into a gallop. She heard Khalis laugh as he matched her pace.

'Are we racing?' he shouted to her, his words torn away on the wind.

'I think we are,' she called back and leaned low over her horse, her heart singing. It felt so good to be free.

The horses' hooves churned up damp sand and her hair streamed out behind her as they raced down the beach. Grace saw a rocky inlet ahead and knew instinctively that it would be their finish line. Khalis pulled ahead and she urged her own mount onwards so they were neck and neck, both of them laughing. In the last moment Grace pulled ahead by half a length and the mare jumped neatly over the scattering of rocks that had comprised their impromptu finish line.

Laughing, she wheeled her mount around and brushed her hair from her eyes. 'I hope you didn't let me win.'

'Never.'

Khalis looked so utterly at ease on his mount, his eyes flashing humour, his skin like burnished gold in the sunlight, that Grace suddenly felt quite dizzy with longing. She knew there was no way she'd won on her own merit, not when she hadn't ridden in over a decade, and Khalis probably having grown up on a horse. Again it didn't matter. Nothing mattered but this day, this one perfect golden day Khalis was giving her, a gift. 'Liar,' she said, smiling, and slipped off the horse. 'But I'll still take the victory. It felt so good to race like that. I'd forgotten how much I like riding.'

'I'm glad you rediscovered it,' Khalis said. He smiled as he brushed a tendril of hair away from her face and her stomach dipped in response to that casual touch. She stood there, blinking up at him, unable to move away. She might as well ask him out loud to touch her again. To kiss her.

He didn't, though, just led their horses up the beach to where the groom was waiting; he must have driven there to meet them. The groom took control of the horses and Khalis reached for Grace's hand. She let him lace his fingers with hers, reminded herself that just for today it was allowed. Today was separate from the rest of her life, alone on this island with a man she could so easily fall in love with.

The thought jolted her, made her hand tense in Khalis's. She couldn't fall in love, not with Khalis, not with anyone. She'd half-convinced herself that she could have this day—just one day—and she would walk away with no one the wiser, her heart intact. But to fall in love? That surely could only mean heartbreak...and discovery.

'Come,' Khalis said. 'Our picnic is waiting.'

He led her to a secluded little cove surrounded by rocks, a blanket already spread across the sand and a basket waiting. Grace gave a soft laugh. 'This took some planning.'

'A little,' he allowed. 'It's easy when you have staff.'

'I can only imagine.'

He drew her down to the blanket and Grace tucked her legs underneath her. Khalis opened the basket and withdrew a bottle of champagne and two glasses. 'A toast,' he said, and popped the cork.

Grace accepted the glass, pushing away the reservations and regrets that still crouched in the corners of her mind. She wasn't falling in love; she was stronger than that. She just wanted to enjoy this moment. This brief and fragile happiness.

'What are we toasting?' she asked.

'To a perfect day,' Khalis suggested.

'To a perfect day,' she echoed, and drank. As she low-

ered her glass she felt Khalis's gaze rest heavily upon her.
'One perfect day,' she said, and she knew she was reminding herself as well as him.

Khalis watched Grace drink, enjoyed the sight of her looking happy and relaxed, her hair tousled and free, her face
flushed with pleasure. He still saw the fear and sadness
lurking in her eyes, and he longed to banish those shadows—not just for one day, but for ever. The fervent nature
of his own thoughts didn't alarm him any more, which surprised him. He was ready for this. Over the years he'd had
a couple of serious relationships, yet he'd never found a
woman who really reached him before. Who touched him
and made him say and feel things he hadn't to anyone else.
Not until Grace.

From the moment he'd met her he'd been intrigued by
her. But he felt more for her than a mere fascination…
He admired her dedication to her career, her strength of
purpose. He sensed, like him, she was a survivor. And
he ached not just to touch her—although he certainly felt
that—but to see her smile and hear her laugh.

Smiling, he reached over and plucked the glass from
her fingers. 'Ready to eat?'

'OK.'

He fed her strawberries and slices of succulent melon,
ripe juicy figs and the softest bread dipped in nutty olive
oil. He loved watching her eat, loved to see her finally enjoying herself, the lines of strain around her mouth and
eyes relaxing at last. He loved the sensuality of feeding
her, of watching her lips part, her eyes widen, her pupils
dilate. It felt quite unbearably erotic.

She finally shook her head, refusing the last lone straw-
berry, her lips still red from the juice. 'You're spoiling me.'

'You deserve to be spoiled.'

The very air around them seemed to tense, freeze. Grace shook her head, her gaze sliding from his. 'No, I don't.'

Khalis had stretched out beside her on the blanket, one arm pillowing his head, and with the other he wound a tendril of soft blond hair around his finger. 'Why do you say that?' he asked quietly.

She shook her head, hard enough for that silky tendril to slip from his finger. 'It doesn't matter.'

He wanted to tell her that it did matter, that everything about her mattered to him, but he swallowed down the words. She wasn't ready to hear them, and perhaps he wasn't ready to say them. Whatever existed between them now was too new and fragile to test it with brash proclamations. Like her, he wanted to enjoy this day. They had plenty of time to learn about each other—learn to trust and maybe even to love—after today. Today—this perfect day—was just the beginning.

Grace watched as Khalis reached for her hair again, winding one silky strand around his finger. He did it almost without thinking, the gesture so relaxed and sure, and yet that simple little touch rocked her to her very core. She shouldn't even feel it—hair, after all, was made up of dead cells, with no nerves. Yet while the scientific part of her brain was reciting these dusty facts, her body blazed to life.

She felt it. Forget science, forget reality, she felt it. She gazed up at him, her eyes wide as she drank him in, his bronzed skin and grey-green eyes now crinkled at the corners as his sensual mouth curled into a knowing smile. Grace's whole body tingled as awareness stole through her, a certain and lovely knowledge that he was going to kiss her.

He lowered his lips to hers slowly, one hand still fisted in her hair as his mouth came down on hers. Her hands slid along his sun-warmed shoulders to clench in the softness of his hair. He lifted his mouth from hers a fraction and his smile deepened; she could *feel* that smile. 'You taste like strawberries.'

She smiled back. 'So do you.'

He let out a little huff of laughter and lowered his head so his mouth claimed hers once more. Grace revelled in that kiss, in this moment, for surely nothing had never been so pure or perfect. Khalis kissed his way slowly along her jawline to the nape of her neck; she let out a sound that was something between a shudder and a laugh as his lips tickled that sensitive spot. He moved lower, to the neckline of her T-shirt, his tongue flicking along her skin, and he tugged it down to press a kiss against the vee between her breasts. Grace arched upwards, her body unfurling like a flower in the sun.

Khalis slid a hand along her waist, his seeking fingers lifting the hem of her T-shirt to touch the sensitized skin beneath. He kissed her again, deeply, and Grace pressed against him. Her own hands sought his skin, tugged up his shirt, slid along the warm, silky stretch of his bare back. She felt his hand slide down along her middle, his palm caressing the tender skin of her tummy.

Behind them a bird suddenly cawed raucously and Grace lurched upright, panic replacing desire. With her clothes in disarray, her hair mussed and her mouth swollen, she felt as if she'd been caught out. Trapped and shamed.

Khalis still reclined on one elbow, looking relaxed. He'd obviously noticed her overreaction, though he said nothing, just let his gaze sweep lazily over her.

'I'm sorry—' she began.

'There's no need to be sorry.'

She let out a shuddering breath. 'I'm not…I haven't…'

'I know.'

He sounded so *sure*, and it made Grace flinch. He didn't know. The assumptions he was making so easily and arrogantly were wrong. Completely, utterly wrong. 'Actually,' she told him, her voice low, 'you don't know.'

'Then tell me.'

No. She tried for a smile. 'We've spent enough time today talking about old memories.'

'That's a brush-off if I've ever heard one.' He didn't sound annoyed, just accepting or perhaps amused. He rolled to a sitting position and began packing the remains of their picnic. Was their perfect day over already?

'We don't have to go yet—'

He touched her heated cheek. 'You're getting sunburn. We're very close to the coast of Africa, you know. The sun is incredibly hot.'

Silently Grace helped him pack up their things. She felt a confused welter of emotions: frustration that the afternoon had ended, as well as relief that it hadn't gone too far. And over it all like a smothering blanket whose weight she'd become so unbearably used to, guilt. Always the guilt.

'Cheer up.' Chuckling softly, Khalis touched her cheek again, his fingers lingering on her skin. 'Don't look so disappointed, Grace. It's only one day.'

Exactly, she wanted to say. Shout. One day—that was all she had. All she'd allow herself, and Khalis knew that. He'd said so himself—hadn't he? Doubt suddenly pricked her. Had she assumed he understood because it was easier to do so? Easier to be blinded by your own desires, to justify and excuse and ignore. But if he didn't understand… if he hadn't accepted her silent, implied terms that today was all they would ever share…what did he want? What did he expect?

Whatever it was, she couldn't give it to him, and a poignant sorrow swept over her as she realised for the first time she wanted to.

CHAPTER SEVEN

WHEN Grace returned to her room she was surprised to find Shayma in attendance, along with an impressive array of clothes and beauty products. Grace stared at a tray of make-up and nail varnish in bewilderment.

'What is all this…?'

Shayma smiled shyly. 'Mr Tannous, he wishes me to help you prepare.'

'Prepare?' Grace turned to gaze at the half-dozen gowns spread out on the bed in bewilderment. 'For what?'

'He is taking you somewhere, I think?'

'Taking me…' Where on earth could he take her to? Not that it mattered; she couldn't go anywhere. She couldn't be seen in public with Khalis, or with any man. Not on a proper date, at least.

'Are they not beautiful?' Shayma said, lifting one of the gowns from the bed. Grace swallowed as she looked at it.

'Gorgeous,' she admitted. The dress was a body-hugging sheath in ivory silk, encrusted with seed pearls. It looked like a very sexy wedding gown.

'And this one as well.' Shayma lifted a dress in a blue so deep it looked black, the satin shimmering like moon-light on water.

'Amazing.' The dresses were all incredible, and she

could not suppress the purely feminine longing to wear one. To have Khalis see her in one.

'And shoes and jewels to match each one,' Shayma told her happily.

Grace shook her head helplessly. She could not believe the trouble and expense Khalis had gone to. She could not believe how much she wanted to wear one of the gowns, and go on a date—a proper date—with him.

See how it happens? her conscience mocked her. *Temptation creeps in, slithers and stalks. And before you know it you're doing things you never, ever thought you'd do. And telling yourself it's OK.*

She knew the rules of her agreement with Loukas. No inappropriate behaviour. No dating. No men. It wasn't fair or really even legal, but in the four years since her divorce she hadn't really cared about the restrictions Loukas had placed upon her. Her heart had its own restrictions. Don't trust. Don't love. *Don't lose yourself.* She hadn't wanted any of it—until Khalis. Khalis made her long to feel close to someone again, to feel the fire of physical desire and the sweetness of shared joy. For the first time in four years she was tempted to let someone in. To trust him with her secrets.

Grace turned away from the sight of those tempting dresses. It was impossible, she reminded herself. Even if her contrary heart had changed, the conditions of her custody arrangement had not.

'Miss...?' Shayma asked hesitantly, and Grace turned back with an apologetic smile.

'I'm sorry, Shayma. I can't wear any of these dresses.'

Shayma stared at her in confused dismay. 'You do not like them?'

'No, I love them all. But I'm not... I can't go out with Mr Tannous.' Shayma looked more confused, and even worried. Grace patted her hand. 'Don't worry. I'll explain to him myself.'

She took a moment to brush her hair and steel herself before heading towards the part of the compound that housed Khalis's study.

Khalis sat behind his desk, and he smiled as she came in. 'I need to tell you—'

He held up one hand. 'You'd like to thank me for the dresses, but you won't go out with me tonight.'

Grace stopped short. 'How did you know?'

'I'd expect nothing less from you, Grace. Nothing about you is easy.'

She bristled; she couldn't help it. 'I'm not sure why you bother, then.'

'I think you do. We share something unusual, something profound—don't we?' He didn't sound remotely uncertain. Grace said nothing, but her silence didn't seem to faze Khalis in the least. 'I've never felt that before with any woman, Grace. And I don't think you've felt it with any man.' He paused, his gaze intent and serious. 'Not even your ex-husband.'

She swallowed. Audibly. And still didn't speak.

'You fascinate me, Grace. You make me feel alive and open and *happy*.'

Grace shook her head slowly. Did he know what his heartfelt confessions did to her? How hungry and heartbroken they made her feel? 'I'm really not that fascinating.'

He smiled wryly. 'Perhaps I'm easily fascinated, then.'

'Perhaps you're easily misguided.'

He arched an eyebrow, clearly surprised by this turn in the conversation. 'Misguided? How?'

Her throat tightened around the words she couldn't say. 'You don't really know me,' she said softly.

'I'm getting to know you. I want to know you.' She shook her head again, unwilling to explain that she didn't want him to get to know her. She didn't want him to know. 'Why won't you go out with me tonight?'

'As I've told you before, I can't.'

'Can't,' Khalis repeated musingly. His body remained relaxed, but his gaze was hard now, unyielding, and Grace knew she would bend beneath that assessing stare. She would break. 'Are you afraid of your ex-husband?'

'Not exactly.'

'Stop talking in riddles.'

Grace knew she'd prevaricated long enough. Khalis had been gentle, patient, kind. He deserved a little honesty. Just a little.

'I have a daughter,' she said quietly. 'Katerina. She's five years old.'

Khalis's expression didn't change, not really, beyond the slight flare of realisation in his eyes, turning them darker, more grey than green, like the ice that covered a lake. You had no idea how hard or thick it was until you stepped on it, let it take your full weight. And then heard the resounding crack in the air as it broke beneath you.

'And?' he finally asked softly.

'My ex-husband has custody of her. I get to see her once a month.'

She could almost hear the creak of the ice, the cracks like spiderwebs splintering the solid ground beneath them. What Khalis had *thought* was solid ground. 'Why is that?' he asked, his tone carefully neutral.

She swallowed, words sticking in her throat, jagged shards of truth she could not dislodge. 'It's complicated,' she whispered.

'How complicated?'

'He's a very powerful and wealthy man,' she explained,

choosing each word with agonised care. 'Our marriage was…troubled and…and our divorce acrimonious. He used his influence to win complete custody.' Her throat closed up over those unsaid jagged shards so they cut her up inside, although surely they'd already done all their damage? She'd lived with the loss of her daughter and her own painful part in it for four years already. Yet it hurt more to tell Khalis now because she never spoke of it. Never to anyone she cared about. And she cared about Khalis. She'd tried not to, still wished she didn't, but she couldn't deny the truth he'd spoken. They did share something. She felt her mouth wobble and tried to look away.

Khalis walked towards her, his expression softening, a sad smile tipping the corners of his mouth. 'Oh, Grace.' She closed her eyes, not wanting to see the undeserved compassion in his gaze. He put his arms around her though she didn't lean into his embrace as she longed to. 'I'm sorry.'

'It was my fault…partly…' A big part.

Khalis brushed this aside, his arms tightening around her. 'Why didn't you fight the custody arrangement? Most judges are inclined favourably towards the mother—'

Except when the mother was thought to be unfit. 'I… couldn't,' she said. At least that was true. She hadn't possessed the strength or courage to fight a judgement her heart had felt was what she deserved.

Khalis tipped her chin up so she had to face him. He looked so tender it made her want to cry. To blurt out the truth—that she didn't deserve his compassion or his trust, and certainly not his love. 'What does this have to do with you and me?'

You and me. How she wanted to believe in that idea. 'Loukas—my ex-husband monitors my behaviour. He's made it a requirement that I don't become…romantically involved with any man. If I do, I lose that month's visit with Katerina.'

Khalis drew back and stared at her in complete bafflement. 'But that…that has to be completely illegal. And outrageous. How can he control your behaviour to such an absurd degree?'

'He has the trump card,' Grace said. 'My daughter.'

'Grace, surely you could fight this. With a *pro bono* solicitor if money is an issue. There's no way he should be able to—'

'No.' She spoke flatly, although her heart raced and her stomach churned. What on earth had possessed her to tell him so much—and yet so little? Now he'd paint her as even more of a victim. 'No, don't, please, Khalis. Leave it. Let's not discuss this any more.'

He frowned, shaking his head. 'I don't understand—'

'Please.' She laid a hand on his arm, felt the corded muscles leap beneath her fingers. 'Please,' she said again, her voice wobbling, and his frown deepened. She thought he'd resist, keep arguing and insisting she fight a battle she knew she'd already lost, but then he sighed and nodded.

'All right. But I'd still like you to go out with me.'

'After what I just told you?'

Smiling, although his eyes still looked dark and troubled, he reached for her hand and kissed her fingers. 'I understand you can't be seen in public with me—yet. But we can still go out.'

She felt the brush of his lips against her fingers like an electric current, jolting right through her and short-circuiting her resolve. She longed to open her hand and press it against his mouth, feel the warmth of his breath against her flattened palm. Step closer so her breasts brushed his chest. With the last vestiges of her willpower she drew her hand back and dredged up a response. 'Go out where?'

'Out there.' He gestured towards the window, the wall. 'Away from this wretched compound.'

'But where—?'

'Grace.' He cut her off, stepping closer so she could feel the intoxicating heat of his nearness and knew her resolve was melting clean away. 'Do you trust me,' he asked, 'to take you somewhere your ex-husband could never discover? A place where you'll be completely safe—with me?'

She stared at him, fear and longing clutching at her chest. One day. One date. It had been four long years and she'd never, *never* known a man like Khalis—a man so gentle he made her ache, so kind he made her cry. A man who made her burn with need. She nodded slowly. 'All right. Yes. I trust you.'

His mouth curled in a smile of sensual triumph and he reached for her hand, kissed her fingers again. 'Good. Because I really would like to take you out to dinner. I'd like to see you in one of those dresses, and I'd like to peel it slowly from your body as I make love to you tonight.' He gave her a wry smile even as his gaze seared straight into her soul. 'But I'll settle for dinner.'

The images he'd conjured brought her whole body tingling to life. 'I can't imagine a place where we can go to dinner that's not—'

'Leave that to me.' He released her hand. 'You can spend some time being spoiled by Shayma.' He pressed a quick, firm kiss against her mouth. 'We'll have a wonderful evening. I'm looking forward to seeing which gown you pick.'

Two hours later, having been massaged and made-up and completely pampered, Grace was dressed in the dress of deep blue satin. She'd wanted to wear the ivory gown, but it had looked too bridal for her to feel comfortable wearing it. She wasn't innocent enough for that dress.

In any case, the blue satin was stunning, with its halter top and figure-hugging silhouette before it flared out in a spray of paler blue at her ankles. Shayma had fastened a diamond-encrusted sapphire pendant around her neck and given her matching earrings as well. She felt like a movie star.

'You look beautiful, miss,' Shayma whispered as she handed Grace her gauzy wrap and Grace smiled her thanks.

'You've been wonderful to me, Shayma. It's been one of the most relaxing afternoons I've had in a long time.'

Khalis was waiting for her at the bottom of the staircase, and he blinked up at her for a moment before he gave her a wide, slow smile of pure masculine appreciation. 'You look,' he told her, reaching for her hand, 'utterly amazing.'

'You look rather nice yourself.' He wore a suit in charcoal-grey silk, but Grace knew he'd look magnificent in anything. He was, simply and utterly, an incredibly attractive man. The suit emphasised the lean, whipcord strength of his body, its restrained power. 'So where are we going?'

'You'll see.'

He led her by the hand out of the compound, through the forbidding gates and then towards the beach. Night was already settling softly on the island, leaving deep violet shadows and turning the placid surface of the sea to an inky stretch of darkness.

Khalis led her to a launch where an elegant speedboat bobbed gracefully in the water. 'We're going by boat?' Grace asked a bit doubtfully, glancing down at her floor-length evening gown. 'I hate to tell you, but I'm feeling a bit overdressed.'

'Well, you look magnificent.' He helped her into the boat, taking care to keep the hem of her gown from trailing in the water. 'I will confess, I had an elegant little hotel in Taormina in mind when I originally had those gowns brought over. But it doesn't really matter where we go, does it? I just want to be with you.' He smiled at her, and Grace's heart twisted.

You're saying all the right things, she wanted to cry. *All the sweet, lovely things any woman wants to hear, and the worst part is I think you mean them.* That was what hurt.

'I am curious,' she murmured, 'where this secret place of yours is.' And nervous. And even afraid. In the four years since her divorce, she'd lost her monthly visits with Katerina twice. Once for going out for a coffee with a colleague, and another time for being asked to dance at a charity function she'd attended for work. She'd refused, but it hadn't mattered. Loukas just liked to punish her.

Khalis headed towards the helm and within a few minutes he was guiding the boat through the sea, the engine purring to life and thrumming beneath them. Grace sat behind a Plexiglas shield, but even so her careful chignon began to fall into unruly tendrils, whipped by the wind.

'Oh, dear.' She held her hands up to her hair, but Khalis just grinned.

'I like seeing you with your hair down.'

She arched her eyebrows. 'Is that a euphemism?'

His grin turned wicked. 'Maybe.'

Laughing a little, feeling far too reckless, she took the remaining pins out of her hair and tossed them aside. Her hair streamed out behind her in a windblown tangle. She probably looked a fright but she didn't care. It felt good. She felt free.

'Excellent,' Khalis said, and the boat shot forward as he accelerated.

Grace still had no idea where they could be going. All around them was an endless stretch of sea, and as far as she knew there were no islands between Alhaja and Sicily. And he couldn't be taking her to Sicily, could he? He'd said somewhere private; he'd asked her to trust him. And she did, even if her stomach still churned with nerves.

'Don't worry,' Khalis told her. 'Where we're going is completely private. And it won't take long to get there.'

'How,' she asked ruefully, 'do you always seem to know what I'm thinking?'

He paused, considering. 'I'd say your every emotion is reflected in your face, but it isn't. It just feels that way.'

Her heart seemed to turn right over. She knew what he meant. Even at his most carefully expressionless, she felt as if she knew what Khalis was feeling, as if she could feel it, too, as if they were somehow joined. Yet they weren't, and in twenty-four hours it would be over. The connection would be severed.

Unless...

For a brief blissful moment she imagined how it could go on. How she'd tell Khalis everything and somehow they'd find a way to fight the custody arrangement. Was this connection they shared strong enough for that?

She glanced at Khalis, her gaze taking in his narrowed eyes, the hard line of his cheek and jaw as he steered the boat. She thought of how he refused to grieve for his family. Forgive his father. Under all the grace and kindness he'd shown her she knew there was an inflexible hardness that had carried him as far as he'd got. A man like that might love, but he wouldn't forgive.

She swallowed, those brief hopes blown away on the breeze like so much ash. They'd been silly dreams, of course. Happy endings. Fairy tales.

'You look rather deep in thought,' Khalis said. He'd

throttled back so the noise of the engine was no more than a steady purr, and Grace could hear the sound of the waves slapping against the sides of the boat.

'Just thinking how beautiful the sea is.' *And how, now that I want to live and love again, I can't.* Khalis had been right. Life wasn't fair, and it was her own fault.

'It is, isn't it?' Khalis agreed, but Grace had the distinct feeling that she hadn't fooled him, and he knew she'd been thinking about something else. About him.

'So are we almost there yet?' she asked, peering out into the unrelieved darkness. A sudden thought occurred to her. 'Are we…are we going to stay on the boat?'

Khalis chuckled. 'You think that's my big surprise? Sausages over a propane stove on a motorboat? I'm almost offended.'

'Well, it is a rather nice boat,' Grace offered.

'Not that nice. And I don't fancy eating my dinner on my lap, bobbing in the water. Come on.' He held out his hand and, surprised, Grace took it. She couldn't see much in the darkness, the only light from the moon cutting a pale swathe of silver across the water. She had no idea where Khalis might be taking her.

He led her to the front of the boat and, even more surprised, Grace realised they had come up next to a small and seemingly deserted island. A slender curve of pale beach nestled against a tangle of foliage, palm fronds drooping low into the water.

'What is this place?'

'A very small, very secluded island my father happened to own. It's not very big at all—a couple of hundred metres across. But my father valued his privacy, and so he bought all the land near Alhaja, even if it wasn't much bigger than a postage stamp.' He vaulted out of the boat easily and then held out his hand to her. 'Come on.'

Grace reached for his hand, teetering a bit in her high heels and long dress, until Khalis put both of his hands firmly on her waist and swung her down off the boat onto the beach. Her heels sunk a good two inches into the damp sand and, ruefully, she slipped them off.

'I think these are designer. I don't want to get them ruined.'

'Much more sensible,' Khalis agreed and kicked his own shoes off. Grace looked at the empty stretch of dark, silent beach, the jungle dense and impenetrable behind it. Everything was very still, and it almost felt as if they were the only two people in the entire world, or at least the Mediterranean.

She turned to Khalis with a little laugh. 'Now I really feel overdressed.'

'Feel free to take your clothes off if you'd be more comfortable.'

Her heart rate skittered. 'Maybe later.'

'Is that a promise?'

Grace gave a little smile. She couldn't believe she was actually *flirting.* And it felt good. 'Definitely not.'

She picked up her dress and held it about her knees as she picked her way across the sand. She hadn't felt so relaxed and even happy in a long, long time. 'So we're not having sausages on the boat. A barbecue on the beach?'

'Wrong again, Ms Turner.' Grinning, Khalis reached for her hand. 'Come this way.' He led her down the darkened beach, towards a sheltered inlet. Grace stopped in surprise at the sight that awaited her there. A tent, its sides rippling in the breeze, had been set up, its elegant interior flickering with torchlight.

It was a tent, but it was as far from propane stoves and camping gear as could be possible. With the teakwood table, silken pillows and elegant china and crystal, it looked like something out of an *Arabian Nights* fantasy.

'How,' Grace asked, 'did you arrange this in the space of a few hours?'

'It was easy.'

'Not that easy.'

'It did take some doing,' Khalis allowed as he reached for the bottle of white wine chilling in a silver bucket. 'But it was worth it.'

Grace accepted a glass of wine and glanced around at the darkness stretching endlessly all about them, co-cooned as they were in the tent with the flickering light casting friendly shadows. Safe. She was safe. And Khalis had made it happen. 'Thank you,' she said softly.

Khalis gazed at her over the rim of his wine glass, his gaze heavy-lidded with sensual intent and yet also so very sincere. 'Thank you,' he said, 'for trusting me.'

'Finally,' she said, and he smiled.

'It didn't take as long as all that.' He started to serve them both hummus and triangles of pitta bread. 'So you must live a very quiet life, with these restrictions your ex-husband has placed on you.'

'Fairly quiet. I don't mind.'

He gave her a swift, searching glance. 'Don't you? I would.'

'You can get used to things.' She'd rather talk about anything else. 'And sometimes,' she half-joked, 'I think I prefer paintings to people.'

'I suppose paintings never let you down.'

'Oh, I don't know,' she said lightly, 'a few paintings have let me down. I once found what I thought was a genuine Giotto in someone's attic, only to discover it was a very good forgery.'

'Isn't it interesting,' Khalis mused, 'how a painting that

looks exactly like the original is worth so much less? Both are beautiful, yet only one has value.'

'I suppose it depends on what you value. The painter or the painting.'

'Truth or beauty.'

Truth. It always came back to truth. The weight of what she wasn't telling him felt as if it would flatten her. Grace took a sip of her wine, tried to swallow it all down. 'Some forgeries,' she said after a moment, 'are worth a fair amount.'

'But nothing like the original.'

'No.'

She felt her heart race, her palms slick, even though they were having an innocuous conversation about art. Except it didn't feel innocuous because what Khalis didn't know—or maybe he already suspected—was that Grace herself was the most worthless forgery of all.

An innocent woman. A maligned wife. Both false, no matter what he thought or how she appeared. No matter what he seemed determined to believe.

'Come and eat,' he said, gesturing to the seat across from him, and Grace went forward with relief. Perhaps now they could talk about something else.

'Had you ever been to this island before?' she asked, dipping a triangle of pitta bread into the creamy hummus. 'As a boy?'

'My brother and I sailed out here once.'

'Once?'

He shrugged. 'We didn't do much together. Everything was a competition to Ammar, one he had to win. And I started not to like losing.' He smiled wryly, but there was something hard about the twist of his lips, a darker emotion that hinted at more than the average sibling rivalry.

'Do you miss him?' Grace asked quietly. 'Your brother, at least, if not your father?'

Khalis's face tensed, his body stilling. 'I already told you I don't.'

'I just find it hard to understand.' Why she felt the need to press, she couldn't say. It was the same kind of compulsion as picking a scab or probing a sore tooth. To see how much it hurt, how much pain you could endure. 'I miss my parents even now—'

'My family was very different from yours.'

'What about your sister? You must miss her.'

'Yes,' Khalis said after a moment. 'I do. But there's no point in going on about it. She's been dead fourteen years.'

He spoke so flatly, so coldly, that Grace could not keep from blurting out, 'How can you... How can you just draw a line across your whole family?'

For a second Khalis's face hardened, his eyes narrowing, lips thinning, and Grace had to look away. This was the man of unrelenting, iron control. The man who never looked back. Never forgave.

'I haven't drawn a line, as you say,' he said evenly, 'across my whole family. I simply see no point in endlessly looking back. They're dead. I've moved on. From mourning them and from this conversation.' He leaned forward, his tone softening. 'My father and brother don't deserve your consideration. You are innocent, Grace, but if you knew the kinds of things they'd done—'

'I'm not as innocent as you seem to think I am.'

'I'm sorry, I don't mean to sound patronising. And I did not intend to talk about my family tonight. Surely there are better ways for us to spend our time.'

'I'm sure there are,' Grace agreed quietly. Why had she pressed Khalis when she had not wanted to talk about her own past? She'd wanted to enjoy herself tonight, and losing themselves in dark memories was not the way to do it.

Khalis served her the next course and she watched the firelight flicker over his golden skin, saw the strength of the corded muscles in his wrist as he ladled fragrant pieces of chicken and cardamom onto her plate. Suddenly the memory of this afternoon, of Khalis's lingering kiss, his hand sliding along her skin, rose up so Grace's whole body broke out into a prickly heat, every muscle and nerve and sinew remembering how heartbreakingly wonderful it had felt when he'd touched her.

She felt her face heat and she reached for her glass. Khalis smiled, his eyes glinting knowingly. 'I think we are both thinking of one way in particular we could spend our time.'

'Probably,' Grace managed, nearly choking on her wine. She could imagine it all too well.

'Let us eat.' The food was delicious, the evening air warm and sultry, the only sound the whisper of the waves against the sand and the rattle of the wind in the palms. Khalis moved the conversation to more innocuous subjects, and Grace enjoyed hearing about how he had built up his business, his life in San Francisco. Khalis asked her about her own life, too, and she was happy to describe her job and some of her more interesting projects. It felt wondrously simple to sit and chat and laugh, to enjoy herself without worry or fear. She'd been living too long under a cloud, Grace thought. She'd needed this brief foray into the light.

All too soon they'd finished their main course and were lingering over thick Turkish-style coffee Khalis had boiled in a brass pot and dessert—a sinful tiramisu—as the stars winked above them and were reflected below upon a placid sea. Grace didn't want the night to end, the magic to stop, for it surely felt like a fantasy, wearing this gown, gazing at the sea, being with Khalis on this enchanted island.

Yet it didn't have to end...not yet, anyway. Her body both tingled in anticipation and shivered with trepidation as she imagined how this magical night could continue. How Khalis could fulfil his promise and slip this gown from her shoulders. Make love to her...as she wanted him to.

Her fingers trembled and she returned her coffee cup to its saucer with a clatter. It had been so long since she'd been with a man. So long since she'd allowed herself the intimacy and vulnerability of being desired. Loved. It scared her still, but she also wanted it. More than she ever had before.

'Why do you look afraid?' Khalis asked quietly. 'We're safe here.' Grace heard both tender amusement and gentle concern in his voice and he reached over to cover her hand with his own.

'I'm not afraid.' She lifted her head to meet his gaze directly, even boldly. She was not afraid, not of him anyway, and not even of Loukas. There was no way he could discover her here. No, she was afraid of herself, and this intense longing that had seized her body and mind and maybe even her heart. Tomorrow she would have to walk away from it.

'Do you wish to return to Alhaja now?'

'Not unless we have to.' She smiled, her eyebrows arched even as her heart thudded. 'Do we?'

'No,' Khalis said in a low thrum of a voice. 'We could stay here.'

Grace didn't know if he meant a little longer or all night. She glanced at a large pillow of crimson and cream striped silk, the torchlight shimmering off the rich material. It looked incredibly soft and inviting, and she could imagine sleeping on it. She could also imagine *not* sleeping on it.

'More coffee?'

She shook her head. 'No, thank you.' Impulsively she leaned forward. 'Let's dance.'

Khalis raised his eyebrows. 'Dance?'

'Yes, dance. On the beach.' The idea had come to her suddenly; this was a date, the only date she'd ever have, and she wanted to enjoy it. She wanted to do all the things she was never able to do because of Loukas and his restrictions. She wanted to dance with Khalis.

A small smile quirked the corner of Khalis's mouth. 'But there's no music.'

Grace held out her arms, gesturing to the rich blue satin of her dress. 'I'm wearing an evening gown on a deserted island. Do we really need music?' She smiled, longing to grab this fragile happiness with both hands. 'Does it really matter?' she echoed his own words back to him.

'Not at all.' In one swift movement Khalis rose from the table and led her out to the beach. The sand was cool and silky beneath her bare feet and the darkness swirled around them, the moon shimmering on the surface of the sea, giving it a fine pearl-like sheen. Khalis turned to her. 'Since there's no music, we can pick the kind we like.'

Grace could hardly see him out here on the dark beach, but she felt the heat and intensity of him, the desire pulsing between them, a sustaining and life-giving force. Impossible to resist. Necessary for life. 'Which kind?' she asked in a voice that sounded a little hoarse.

'Something slow and lazy,' Khalis said. He reached out and pulled her towards him so her hips collided gently with his and heat pooled in her pelvis. She let her hands slide up his shoulders, lace around his neck as he started to sway. 'A saxophone, maybe. Do you like sax?'

'Sax,' Grace repeated dazedly. Khalis had slid his hands from her shoulders to her waist to her hips, and now his fingers were splayed along her bottom as he pulled her even closer, against the full thrust of his arousal. 'I... Yes, I think so.'

'Good,' he murmured, and they swayed silently together. Grace could have sworn she heard music, the lonely wail of a saxophone as they danced on the empty beach, their bare feet leaving damp footprints in the sand.

Above them the sky was scattered with stars, a hundred thousand glittering pin-pricks in an inky, endless sky. Grace laid her head on Khalis's shoulder, felt the steady thud of his heart against her own chest. After a moment she lifted her head and tilted back so she could look up into his eyes. His lips were a whisper away. The sleepy sensuality of the dance was replaced by something far more primal and urgent, something whose force was overwhelming and irresistible.

'Grace,' Khalis said and it almost sounded like a warning.

But Grace didn't want warnings. She didn't want memories or guilt or fear. She just wanted this. 'Khalis,' she whispered and his fingers brushed her cheek.

'I love it when you say my name.'

'I was amazingly resistant to saying it.' She turned her head so her lips brushed his fingers. She felt carefree to the point of wantonness, and after four years of being completely buttoned-up it felt good. Khalis let out a little shudder as her tongue darted out and touched his fingers, tasted the salt of his skin. He took her chin in his hand and gazed down at her with a ferocity that would have frightened her if she hadn't felt it herself.

Then he kissed her hard, so different from the gentle caresses of this afternoon, and yet so right. The very air seemed to ignite around them, the stars exploded in the sky as Grace kissed him back and Khalis pulled her even closer, his mouth moving from her lips to her jaw to her throat and she heard the primal sound of her own desperate moan of longing.

He pressed another kiss in the curve of her neck and she tilted her head back, allowing him access. The feel of his lips against her skin gave her a plunging sensation deep inside, turned her mind into a whirlpool of need.

'This dress is going to get very sandy,' Khalis murmured against her throat and Grace gave a shaky laugh.

'I don't care. Although I suppose you might.' She had to find the words from somewhere deep inside her, for thought of any kind was proving virtually impossible. Khalis had undone the halter top of the dress and was slowly peeling it away from her, just as he'd promised.

'I find,' he murmured as he slid the gown down her body, 'I don't care about this dress at all.'

'It is beautiful,' Grace gasped as he finished removing it and tossed it onto the sand. 'Was,' she amended, and Khalis let out a hoarse laugh as his gaze roved over her.

'Grace, *you* are beautiful. Utterly and shockingly beautiful.'

She should have felt embarrassed, standing in her knickers in the middle of a beach, but she didn't. She wasn't even wearing a bra because she hadn't brought one that fitted the halter-style top of the dress. The cool breeze puckered her bare skin into gooseflesh.

'Shockingly?' she repeated. 'That sounds rather alarming.'

'It is alarming,' Khalis told her. He stepped closer to her, ran his hands lightly over her shoulders before cupping her breasts. His palms were warm and dry and still

Grace shivered under his touch. 'It's alarming to me, what I feel for you,' he said in a low voice.

Grace's heart lurched. Yes, it was alarming to her, too. Terrifying and wonderful at the same time. 'Kiss me,' she murmured, and as Khalis brushed his lips against her own she closed her eyes.

He deepened the kiss, but only for a moment, pulling away from her to brush her lids with his fingers. 'Open your eyes.'

'Wh-what?' Her eyes fluttered open and she stared at him, the mobile curve of his mouth hardening just a little bit as he gazed back at her.

'Don't turn your mind off, Grace. I'm making love to you, body and mind and soul.'

'You don't ask for much, do you?'

'Just everything.' And then he claimed her mouth in a kiss that was as hard and unrelenting as she knew the core of him to be, reminding her that no matter how gentle this man was, how tender and even loving, he was still a dangerous proposition. 'Kiss me back,' he muttered against her mouth, and she did, returning the demand, answering it.

He pulled her closer, her breasts crushed against his chest as his hands slid down the bare expanse of her back and tugged off her knickers. Then, his gaze still locked on hers, he stepped back and reached for the buttons of his own shirt. Mesmerised, Grace watched as he began to undress, her own nakedness almost forgotten as he slid his shirt off and revealed the lean, muscled chest underneath. His skin was golden with a satiny sheen, a light sprinkling of hair veeing down to his waistband. Her breath hitched. Khalis undid his belt.

Seconds later, they were both naked. Grace tried not to shiver. Khalis's heated gaze was enough to fire her body, yet she could not shake the feeling of vulnerability that stole over her and made her cold. She'd forgotten how *intimate* this all was. How revealing. She'd been on her own for so long, buttoned-up and barricaded, protected. Now there was nothing. Now she was bare.

At least physically. Emotionally, Grace knew, she was still as guarded as ever. And now more than ever, as Khalis led her back to the tent and drew her down to the pillows' opulent softness, she wanted to tell the last of her secrets. She wanted to bare her soul. She wanted, Grace knew, to be understood and accepted. Forgiven. *Loved.*

Yet she didn't know how to begin. Her thoughts were a ferment of uncertainty, even as pleasure began to take over.

Khalis trailed kisses from her throat to her tummy and desire dazed her senses, scattering her thoughts. His mouth moved lower, his tongue flicking against her skin, and then, thankfully, she had no more thoughts at all.

Something was missing. Even as he heard Grace's little gasps and mews, even as his own libido ran rampant, Khalis knew it wasn't enough. He wanted more from Grace, more than this physical response, overwhelming as it was. He wanted to destroy the defences she'd put around herself. He wanted her completely open to him, body and mind, heart and soul.

You don't ask for much, do you?

He'd never wanted so much from a woman before, but then he'd never felt so much for a woman before. And yet, even as her body lay naked to him, even as she parted her legs and arched up towards his caress, Khalis knew she was closing off her mind. Her heart.

'Look at me, Grace.'

Her eyes fluttered open, unfocused and dazed with passion. 'What—' He braced himself on his elbows, poised over her as her breath came in little pants. *'Please—'*

He knew what she wanted. God knew he wanted it, too. In one stroke he could be embedded deep inside her and satisfy them both. He stayed still. 'Say my name.'

Confusion clouded her eyes. Her lips parted. 'Why—?'

'Say my name.'

It wasn't much, but it was, at least, a beginning. She would acknowledge him, own this connection between them. He wouldn't let her memories or fears crowd him out. He wouldn't let her try to banish him along with her ghosts. She didn't speak and sweat beaded on his brow. He could not hold himself back much longer. *'Please.'*

Her expression softened and the sudden tears that shimmered in her eyes nearly broke him. 'Khalis,' she whispered, and with a primal groan of satisfaction he drove inside her, felt her welcoming warmth wrap around him. 'Khalis,' she said again, her nails digging into his shoulders, her body arching upwards, and triumph tore through him as they surged towards a climax. Grace cried aloud, her head thrown back as her legs wrapped around him. His name sounded like both a supplication and a blessing as her body convulsed around his. *'Khalis.'*

CHAPTER EIGHT

GRACE lay in the cradle of Khalis's arms and could not keep the tears from silently slipping down her face. She closed her eyes, but still they came, one after the other, tears of poignant joy and bitter regret. She'd never felt so close to a man before…and yet so unbearably far away. She'd been so afraid to open her heart and body and soul to him, afraid of the strength of her own feelings. Right to the end she'd resisted, and then…

Then her heart had cracked right open and instead of feeling like the end it had been a beginning. Life instead of death. Hope instead of fear. How could she not have realised how different it would be with Khalis, how wonderful?

And yet how could it last?

She thought she was crying silently, so Khalis, his arms wrapped around her as he drew her back against his chest, wouldn't hear, but he did. Or perhaps he just sensed it, as he had so many other things. Gently his hands came up towards her face and his thumbs wiped away her tears. Neither of them spoke. After a long moment Grace drew in a shuddering breath, her face still damp although at least the tears had stopped.

Khalis pressed a kiss against her shoulder, his arms still wrapped around her. 'Tell me,' he said quietly.

Grace closed her eyes. Another tear leaked out. She wanted to tell him, tell him everything about her disastrous marriage, her own stupid, selfish folly, her painful divorce, the endless aftermath. She'd given him the barest of details, made herself look far more of a victim than she was. Now she imagined telling him all of it, having every sordid secret spill out of her, and while it would be a relief, like a blood-letting, it would also be messy and painful. And it would change the way Khalis looked at her. Why that should even matter since she didn't intend to see him again after tonight, Grace couldn't say. It just did.

She drew a deep breath and rolled over onto her back, Khalis's arm heavy across her. 'It's just been a long time,' she said, attempting a smile. 'I'm kind of emotional.'

Khalis studied the tracks Grace knew her tears had made down her face. 'You're sad.'

'And happy.' She pressed a kiss against his palm. 'Very happy.'

Khalis didn't look convinced but, to Grace's relief, he let it go. He pulled her more securely against him and she lay there for a long time, his arms wrapped around her as she stared into the darkness, savouring the steady warmth of him next to her, the reassuring rise and fall of his chest. Eventually she slept.

When she woke the tent was washed in sunlight and Khalis was gone. She knew he couldn't have gone far—they were on a deserted island, after all—and so for a few seconds she just lay there against the pillows, recalling the sweet memories, enjoying this brief happiness. Then she rose, wrapping a cashmere throw around her, for her gown—the only clothes she'd brought—was lying discarded and damp on the sand some metres away.

Khalis appeared, coming from the beach, looking energised and alert, a towel slung low round his hips. His hair was damp and spiky, and when he smiled Grace started to melt.

'Good morning.'

'Good morning. You had a dip in the sea?'

'A very refreshing way to start the day,' he confirmed. 'Sleep well?'

'Yes.'

'It took you a long time to go to sleep.'

Surprised, her grip loosened and the throw slid down revealingly. She hitched it up again. 'How did you know that?'

'I just sensed it, I suppose.'

'It felt strange to sleep next to someone,' Grace admitted. 'But nice.'

'Good.' Without a modicum of self-consciousness, Khalis dropped his towel and began to dress. Grace watched as he pulled on a pair of faded jeans, his legs long, lean and sprinkled with dark hair. 'Where did you get those clothes?' she asked, more to distract herself from the sight of his naked body than any real sense of curiosity.

'I brought a bag with a change of clothes for both of us.' He gave her a quick grin. 'Just in case.'

'Rather confident, weren't you?' she said, smiling and blushing at the same time.

'I like to be prepared.' He reached for a T-shirt and Grace leaned back against the pillows and watched him dress. It was a glorious sight. 'I thought we could have a look round the island this morning,' he said as he fastened his jeans. 'Not that there's much to see.'

'That sounds nice.' Anything to extend their time together.

Khalis sat down next to her on the pillow, his expression turning serious. He rested one hand on her knee. 'And tonight I want to fly back to Paris with you.'

Shock rendered her momentarily speechless. 'You… what?'

'I put a call in to the head of my legal team,' Khalis continued, 'and asked him a few questions. There's no way this custody arrangement is legal, Grace. We can fight it. We might even be able to dig something up on Christofides. I don't think he's squeaky clean. My team is researching it now—'

Grace just stared at him, her mind frozen. 'How did you know his last name?' she asked. 'I never told you.'

'I did some research.'

'I thought you didn't like internet stalking.'

His expression hardened. 'Sometimes it's justified.'

She let out a short laugh. 'Is it?'

'What's wrong, Grace? I thought you'd be happy to hear this. I want to fight for you. And your daughter.'

She shook her head, wanting to deny the fierce hope his words caused to blaze within her. 'You should have told me you were doing those things.'

'I wanted to have some information before I said anything—'

'I don't like being bossed around.' Her words came out sharply—sharper than she intended. 'I *really* don't like it.'

Khalis was silent for a moment. 'Is that what he did to you?' he asked quietly. 'Ordered you around? Kept you imprisoned on some island?'

Grace stared at him, the fierce light in his eyes, the hard line of his mouth. 'Something like that.'

'I'm not your ex-husband.'

'I know,' she snapped. This conversation was scraping her emotions raw, making her feel more exposed than ever. Exposed and hidden at the same time, for everything about their relationship was a mess of contradictions. A paradox of pleasure and pain. Secrets and honesty. Hope and despair. She took a deep breath. 'I know,' she said again, more quietly. 'But, Khalis—it's not that simple. You should have told me what you were doing before you interfered.'

'Interfered? I thought I was *helping* you.'

'There are things—' She stopped, bit the inside of her cheek hard enough to taste blood. 'Things I haven't told you.'

'Then tell me. Whatever it is, *tell* me.'

She stared at him, trying to find the words. Form them. A few simple sentences, that was all, but it could change everything. And even now, when she'd lain sated in Khalis's arms and he'd wiped away her tears, she was desperately afraid.

'Grace,' he said quietly and reached for her hand. His hand was warm and dry and strong, and hers felt small and icy in it. Still she didn't speak. 'Whatever it is, whatever happened between you and your husband, I can handle it. I've seen a lot of things in this world. Terrible things.'

'You're talking about your father.'

'Yes—'

'But you walked away from him. From all that.'

'Of course I did.' He was silent for a moment, struggling for words. 'I don't know what your husband did to you,' he said quietly, stroking her fingers, 'but I hate him for it. I'll never forgive him for hurting you.'

Slowly Grace lifted her gaze to his. He looked intent and utterly sincere. He'd meant his words as some kind of comfort, an assurance that he was on her side. He didn't realise just how cold that comfort was. *I'll never forgive him for hurting you. I'll never forgive. Never forgive.* She heard the relentless echo of that hard promise in her mind, and she pulled her hand from his.

'There's no point in discussing this,' she said, and struggled up from the bed of pillows, wished she was wearing more than a cashmere throw. 'Did you say you brought me some clothes?'

Khalis had gone very still, his grey-green stare tracking her movements as she hunted for the bag of clothes. 'Why is there no point?'

With relief Grace pulled a pair of trousers and a T-shirt from a duffel bag. She straightened and turned to face him, the clothes clutched to her hard-beating heart. 'Because I don't want you to fly to Paris with me. I don't want you to call your legal team and tell me what to do. I don't want *you.*' She stared at him, each word a hammer blow to her heart—and his. They were lies, and yet she meant them. This, Grace thought numbly, was the worst contradiction of all: she was breaking the heart of a heartless man. She loved someone who couldn't love her back, even if he thought he did.

He didn't know her.

Khalis didn't answer for a moment. His face was devoid of expression, although the corners of his mouth had whitened. 'I don't believe you,' he said finally.

'Do I have to spell it out for you?'

'You're afraid.'

'Stop telling me what I feel,' Grace snapped. 'Stop deciding just what it is between us. You keep telling me what I feel, as if you know. Well, you don't. You don't know anything.'

'If I don't know something,' Khalis answered, his voice so very even, 'it's because you haven't told me.'

'And maybe I haven't told you because I don't want to,' Grace retorted. How could she feel heartbroken and furious at the same time? She was afraid he'd reject her if she told him the truth, and yet at that moment she was angry enough to reject him. Nothing made sense. 'Just take me back to Alhaja,' she said. 'And then I'll find my way back to Paris myself.'

Anger sparked in Khalis's eyes, turning them golden-green. 'And how will you do that? Swim?'

'If I have to,' Grace flashed back. 'If you think you can keep me on that damned island—'

'I told you before,' he cut her off icily, 'I am *not* your ex-husband.'

'There's a startling resemblance at the moment.' As soon as she said the words Grace knew she didn't mean them. Khalis was nothing like Loukas. He'd been so gentle and kind and *loving*, and she was the one pushing him away. Pushing him away because she didn't want to be pushed away first. *Coward.*

The silence between them felt taut with suppressed fury. Khalis stared at her for a long moment, his face unreadable, his chest heaving. He drew a deep breath, and Grace watched as he focused his anger into something cold and hard. 'I thought,' he said, staring into the distance, his body now angled away from her, 'we had something special. That sounds ridiculously sentimental, I know. I didn't really believe in *special* until I felt it with you.' He turned to face her and Grace flinched from the bleakness in his eyes. 'But all that *we sense each other's emotions* stuff, this connection between us—that was just crap, wasn't it? Complete rubbish.'

Grace didn't answer. She couldn't. She didn't have the strength to deny it, and yet she could not tell him the truth. She wasn't even sure what the truth was any more. How could she fall in love with someone who was so hard and unyielding? How could she truly believe in his gentleness and all the good things he'd shown her? 'There's no point to this conversation,' she finally said flatly. 'We could drag it all out, and do a post-mortem on everything we've ever said, but since we're not going to *have* a relationship—' she drew in a ragged breath '—why bother?'

'Why bother,' he repeated softly. 'I see.'

She forced herself to meet his icy stare. 'Yes,' she said, 'I think you do.'

He stared at her, his face so blank and pitiless. Slowly he shook his head. 'I thought I knew you, or was at least coming to know you, but you're really a stranger, aren't you? A complete and utter stranger.' He might as well have said *bitch* instead. 'I don't know you at all.'

'No,' Grace agreed softly, 'you don't.' She drew in a deep, shuddering breath. 'Now I think you should take me back to Alhaja, and then I'll go home.'

He stared at her, and for a moment he looked like a different man, everything about him hard and unyielding and angry. The core revealed. Grace had known it was there, had known he possessed it, yet that cold, hard fury hadn't been directed at her...until now.

'Fine,' he said shortly. 'I'll get the boat ready.' And in two swift strides he'd left the tent, disappearing down towards the beach.

Khalis didn't speak to her again except for a few terse commands when she boarded the boat. She glanced at him, his jaw bunched as he stared out at the endless blue horizon, and again she felt that ridiculous, desperate longing for things to be different. To tell him everything, to take a chance. Maybe it wouldn't matter. Maybe he'd accept and understand and—

She watched as his eyes narrowed against the now-blazing sun and all the things he'd said tumbled back into her mind. He didn't forgive. He didn't want to forgive. He was a man with high and exacting standards for himself as well as everyone else. She fell far short of them and nothing could change that. Nothing could change the fact that she didn't deserve his love.

Tears thickened in her throat and stung her eyes and, furious with herself, Grace blinked them away. Was she really going to have a pity party *now*? The notion was ludicrous, idiotic. And far too late.

Alhaja Island loomed in the distance, a green crescent-shaped speck, and then the walls with their barbed wire and broken glass became visible, the ugly concrete compound behind.

Khalis docked the boat and cut the engine and in the sudden silence they both sat there, neither speaking or even looking at each other.

'Get your things,' he finally said. 'I'll have someone take you back to Paris.'

'I can get transport from Taormina. If someone could just—'

'I'll get you home,' he told her brusquely. He paused, and as he turned to her Grace saw a welter of emotion in his agate-coloured eyes and its answer rose up in her chest, a silent howl of anguish and loss. If only things could be different. If only *they* were different. His lips twisted in something close to a smile and he lifted his hand, almost as if he were going to touch her. Grace tensed in anticipation and longing, but he didn't, just dropped it back to his side. 'Goodbye, Grace,' he said, and then he vaulted out of the boat and strode down the dock.

Fury drove Khalis to the pool. He needed to work off his frustration…and his pain. Stupid, to feel so hurt, like a kicked puppy. And it was his own damn fault.

He dived in and cut through the water with sure, swift strokes, his emotions driving him forward. Even as he swam he winced. He'd been so sentimental, so stupidly romantic, and she'd been the one to spell it out. *I don't want you.* He felt pathetic. Pathetic and bruised.

He'd blinded himself all along, he knew, turned deaf ears to what she was saying. *I couldn't be in a relationship with you.* He'd thought she was just afraid, wounded by her ex-husband, and maybe she was. Maybe it was fear that had made her reject him, but the fact still remained, hard and heartless. She didn't want him. He'd wanted to rescue her as if she were some princess in a tower, but she didn't want to be rescued. Or loved. And, really, did he even know her at all? How could you fall in love with someone so quickly and suddenly? Wasn't it supposed to grow over months and years, not a mere matter of days?

Khalis completed another lap and hauled himself, dripping, onto the side of the pool. Even now, his chest heaving and his lungs burning, he couldn't get her out of his mind. Those chocolate eyes, dark with pain or softened with humour. Her mouth, swollen and rosy from being kissed. The pure, clear sound of her rare laughter, and the way she looked at him, her attention so focused and complete it made him feel a hundred feet tall. The pliant softness of her body against his, and the way he'd felt when he'd been inside her, as if he'd finally found the home he'd long been looking for.

With a groan of frustration Khalis pushed off the side of the pool and started swimming again, harder and faster than ever, as if exercise could obliterate thought. In the distance he heard the sound of the helicopter taking off.

An hour later, showered and dressed, he strode into his office. His frustration and hurt had hardened into something cold and steely that lodged inside him like a ball of iron.

Eric was waiting for him with a sheaf of papers as he

sat behind his desk. 'You look,' Eric remarked mildly, 'like you want to rip someone's head off. I hope it's not mine.'

'Not at all.' He held out one hand for the papers. Eric handed them to him with his eyebrows arched.

'If not me, then who?' He rolled his eyes. 'Wait, I think I can guess.'

'Don't,' Khalis said, cutting him off. 'It's not up for discussion.'

'This island is really doing a number on you, isn't it?'

Khalis suppressed his irritation with effort. Eric was one of his oldest and most trusted friends, and he generally appreciated his levity. Yet, since coming to this island, tension had been wrapping itself around him like a steel band, choking all the life and hope from the air. Grace had distracted him, he realised. She'd *helped* him. And her rejection had made everything worse, the memories darker, the pain more intense.

'It's not the island,' he said shortly. 'I'd just like to wrap up this whole business quickly and get back to my real life.' Except he wasn't sure he could do that any more, or at least not easily. Not since Grace.

'I wouldn't mind a few more weeks lounging in the sun,' Eric said, although Khalis knew his assistant had done precious little lounging since arriving on Alhaja. 'Is there anything else for now?'

'No—' Khalis dropped the papers on his desk and raked a hand through his hair. 'Yes,' he amended. 'I want you to find everything you can on Grace Turner.'

'Everything?' Eric asked dubiously. 'You sure you want to go there?'

He gritted his teeth. 'Yes.'

Eric gave him a considering look, then shrugged. 'It's your party,' he said, and left the room. Resolutely, Khalis pulled the papers towards him. Grace had told him he could find out what he needed to know with one simple internet search. Well, he thought grimly, maybe now he'd take her up on that.

By the time Grace arrived back at her apartment in Paris's Latin Quarter, she felt exhausted, both emotionally and physically. Khalis's helicopter had taken her to Taormina, and then he'd arranged a private jet to take her directly to Paris. Even at the end, when he must have hated her, he was considerate. She almost wished he wasn't. When he'd been arrogant and controlling it had been far easier to stay angry and to let that carry her. Then he softened into gentleness and she felt all tangled up inside, yearning and fear tying her heart into knots. Why couldn't he make it easy for her to let go? Simple not to care? Yet nothing about her time with Khalis had been simple or easy.

Yes, it had, she corrected herself. It had been all too easy to fall in love with him.

Resolutely, Grace pushed the useless thought away. She had no space or freedom in her life for love. Khalis might have cracked open her heart, but she could close it again. Love led to pain. She knew that. She'd seen it with Loukas, when he'd left her alone on his island, trapped and miserable, half-mad with loneliness.

And as for Andrew...

No, she wouldn't think about Andrew.

Slowly, each movement aching, she dropped her bag and kicked off her heels. She curled up on the sofa, wishing she could blank out her mind. Stop thinking, stop remembering. Not Loukas or Andrew, but Khalis. Khalis smiling at her, teasing her, making her laugh.

Frankly, that looks like something my five-year-old goddaughter might paint in Nursery.

Even now Grace's mouth curved into a smile as tears

stung her eyes. Khalis looking at her, heavy-lidded with
sensual intent. Kissing her so softly, so sweetly. Finding
ways to make her feel safe and treasured.

Now the tears spilled over and Grace buried her face
in her hands. Had she made a mistake, not trusting him?
If she'd told him what she'd done, would he have forgiven
her? And wasn't loving someone worth that risk?

She drew in a shuddering breath and other memories
came to her. Khalis's eyes narrowed, his mouth a hard,
compressed line.

You're very forgiving, much more forgiving than I am.

No, he wasn't forgiving. And he wouldn't forgive her.
And even if she'd fallen in love with him, it didn't change
who he was. And who she couldn't be.

CHAPTER NINE

GRACE transferred her untouched glass of champagne to her other hand and tried to focus on what the ageing socialite across from her was droning on about. She caught a word here and there and she thought she was making the appropriate noises of interest, but her entire body and brain were buzzing with the knowledge that Khalis would be here tonight. After two months, she would see him again.

Tension coiled through her body, twanging like a wire. She had had no contact with Khalis these last few months, although she'd exchanged a few emails with Eric, arranging for the art collection to be transferred. Khalis had, of course, obeyed all the legal procedures in authenticating the artwork in his father's vault and turning it over to the proper authorities. Tonight was a gala celebrating the return of several important paintings to the Louvre, as well as Khalis's generous donation of a Monet that had been one of the few paintings in his father's collection that had not been stolen.

The party was being held in the Louvre's impressive courtyard, the distinctive glass pyramids glinting in the last rays of the setting sun. It was early summer and the air was sun-warmed and fragrant. Grace took a sip of champagne to ease the dryness in her throat and glanced around the milling crowd for Khalis. He hadn't arrived. She would know it if he had.

And when he did arrive, Grace asked herself yet again, what would she say to him? How would she act? Prudence required that she keep a professional distance, yet two months had only intensified her longing and regret and she was afraid she'd betray herself when she saw him again.

She attempted to turn her attention back to the social-ite, yet within seconds it felt as if someone had suddenly turned a spotlight on her, even though nothing had notice-ably changed. She felt a prickling between her shoulder blades, a tingling awareness creep through her entire body. He was here.

Barely aware of what she was saying, she excused her-self from the conversation and turned away, trying to search the crowds discreetly. It didn't take long; it was as if he were equipped with a tracking device to her heart, for she saw and felt him right away. He stood alone, his figure tall and proud, his gaze sweeping over the crowd. Then that cold gaze fastened on her and Grace's breath hitched. For an endless moment they stared at one another, and from across the crowded courtyard Grace could not discern his expression. She didn't even know what the expression on her own face was, for both body and brain seemed to have frozen.

Then Khalis looked away, his gaze moving on with-out any real acknowledgement of her presence. Head held high, she turned away and walked towards another knot of guests, forced herself to listen to their idle chatter. What had she expected? That Khalis would run over and greet her? Kiss her? She wouldn't even have wanted that. She *couldn't* want that. Yet it still hurt, not the pain of disap-pointment, for Grace hadn't really expected anything from him tonight, but the agony of remembered loss.

Somehow she made it through the next hour, listening and nodding, murmuring platitudes although she barely knew what she was saying. Her body ached with the knowledge of Khalis's nearness and, even without looking, she was certain she knew exactly where he was. Amazing, and still alarming, to share this connection that they'd both acknowledged…and then she'd denied.

The evening dragged, every moment painfully slow as Grace instinctively tracked Khalis's progress around the courtyard. He looked amazing in a dark suit and silver-grey tie, as lean and powerful and darkly attractive as ever, and just glimpsing him out of the corner of her eye reminded her how warm and satiny his skin had been, how complete she'd felt in his arms.

By the end of the social hour, and then another half hour of speeches, she felt ready for bed. Tension knotted in her shoulders and her head pulsed with the beginnings of one of the stress-related headaches she'd been getting ever since her divorce. The party had moved inside to the Pavillon Denon, and Grace stayed near the back of the gallery as the director of the museum praised Khalis's civic service in restoring so many famous works of art to their rightful places. Her heart twisted like a wrung rag inside her when Khalis stepped to the podium and spoke eloquently about his duty 'to redeem what has been forsaken, and find what has been lost'.

Pretty words, Grace thought with a sudden spike of spite, but he hadn't been much interested in redemption when she'd been talking to him. When it came to his father, he'd been cold, hard and unforgiving.

And you were so afraid he'd be the same with you. That's why you ran away like a frightened child.

Not that it mattered. The only child she could think of was Katerina. Just the thought of her daughter's apple-round cheeks, her dark plaits and her gap-toothed smile made Grace blink fiercely. She had to forget about Khalis, for Katerina's sake as well as her own.

The speeches over, Grace excused herself from the party. She saw Michel give her a sharp glance from across the room; she didn't think she'd fooled him since she'd returned from Alhaja.

The rest of the museum was quiet and dark, and it felt strange to be wandering alone among all this priceless art. Of course, everything was wired to a central security system and there were guards at every exit, but Grace at least had the illusion of solitude.

She headed down the stairs, past the ancient statue of Winged Victory of Samothrace, when a voice caused her to still.

'Leaving already?'

She half-turned, saw Khalis coming down the stairs to meet her. 'I wanted some air.' She needed some now, for the sight of him had stolen the breath right from her lungs.

He stopped a foot or so in front of her and in the dim lighting Grace could not quite read his expression. His eyes were narrowed, but whether in concern or anger or mere indifference she could not say. 'Are you getting one of your headaches?'

She shrugged. 'It's been a long day.'

'You look tired.'

'I am.' She wondered why he cared, knew she wanted him to. 'I should go.' Still she didn't move.

'I haven't forgotten you, Grace.' His voice was pitched low, assured and so very sincere. She angled her head away from him, another wave of loss sweeping through her, nearly bringing her to her knees.

'You should have.'

'Have you forgotten me?'

'No, of course not.' She took a step away from him. They shouldn't be here, having this conversation alone.

'Of course not?' Khalis repeated. He'd stepped closer to her, blocking her escape route down the stairs. She glanced back at the statue of Nike, armless and headless yet still magnificent, the only witness to this encounter. 'That surprises me.' She said nothing, unwilling to continue the conversation even as her gaze roved over him, drinking him in, memorising his features. God, she'd missed him. Even now, when he looked so intent and angry, she missed him. Wanted him. 'The last time I saw you,' he said, 'you gave the distinct impression you wanted to forget me.'

'I did want to,' Grace answered. She couldn't be anything but honest now; the sheer closeness and reality of him was too much for her to be able to prevaricate. *Lie.* 'But I couldn't.' He'd stepped closer, so close she could breathe the achingly familiar scent of him, feel his intoxicating heat. She closed her eyes. 'Don't—'

'Don't what? Don't make you remember how good it was between us?' Slowly, deliberately, he reached out one hand and traced the line of her cheek. His thumb touched the fullness of her mouth and Grace shuddered.

'Please—'

'We still have it, Grace. That connection between us. It's still there.'

She opened her eyes, furious and afraid and despairing all at once. 'Yes, it is, but it doesn't matter.'

'You keep saying that, but I don't believe it.'

'I told you—'

'You didn't tell me anything. I'm still waiting for that, Grace. Waiting—and wanting to understand.' She just shook her head, unable to speak. 'I want,' he said, his teeth gritted, 'to give you a second chance—'

And she'd wanted to believe in second chances, even if she couldn't have one. 'Don't, Khalis.'

'You still want me—'

'Of course I do!' she shouted, her nerves well and truly shattered. 'I'm not denying it. So are you happy now? Satisfied?'

'Not in the least.' And, before she could protest or even think, he'd pulled her to him and his mouth came down hard and relentless and yet so very sweet on hers.

Grace gave in to the kiss for a blissful fraction of a second, her hands coming up to grip his shoulders, her body pressed so wonderfully against his, before she jerked away, her chest heaving. *'Don't!'*

Khalis was breathing as hard as she was, his face flushed, his eyes flashing fire. 'Why did you walk away from me?'

Tears pricked her eyes and her head blazed with pain. Truth spilled from her lips. 'Because I was afraid you'd hate me if I stayed.' A sound of someone on the stair above her made Grace's insides lurch in panic. She shook her head, unable to look at him. 'Just leave me alone,' she whispered. *'Please.'*

And then she fled down the stairs.

Back in her apartment, Grace peeled off her cocktail dress and took a long, hot shower, tried to banish the imprint of Khalis's mouth on hers, the blaze of desire his touch had caused her. She couldn't believe he'd still pursued her, still wanted her. She thought he'd hate her by now, and the fact that he didn't made it so much harder to forget him.

After her shower, dressed in her most comfortable worn pyjamas, Grace pulled out the photo album from the top shelf of the bookcase in her bedroom. She tried not to look at this album too often because it hurt too much. Yet tonight she needed to look at the beloved pictures, remind herself just what she had lost—and still had to lose.

Katerina at birth, her face tiny and wrinkled and red. Six weeks old, fast asleep in her pram. Six months, one chubby fist in her mouth, her eyes the same brown as Grace's own. A year, taking her first toddling steps. After that there were no photos except the ones Grace took when she saw her daughter once a month, in Athens. She gazed at these hungrily, as if she could fill in the many missing pieces of her daughter's last four years. Loukas had arranged it perfectly, she thought not for the first time, too weary now to be bitter. She saw Katerina enough for the girl to remember her, but not enough to love her as a child loved her mother. As Grace loved her daughter.

A sharp, purposeful knock on the front door startled her out of her thoughts and quickly she closed the album and slid it back on its shelf. Her heart had begun beating with hard, heavy thuds for she knew who was knocking at her door.

'Hello, Khalis.' Colour slashed his cheekbones and he held his body tensely, like a predator waiting to spring. He looked, Grace thought with a spasm of hopeless longing, as wonderful as always.

'May I come in?'

Wordlessly she nodded and stepped aside so he could enter. Khalis came into her little sitting room with its slanted ceilings and rather shabby antique furniture, seeming to dominate the small space.

To her surprise, he took a pile of folded papers from his inside pocket and dropped them on the coffee table with a thud.

'What is that?'

'Your file.'

'My *file*?'

His mouth tightened. 'After you left, I had Eric research your background.' He gestured to the thick pile of papers. 'He gave me that.'

Grace took in his hard expression, the narrowed eyes and tightened mouth, and she swallowed dryly. She knew what kind of articles the online gossip sites and tabloids had run. Sordid speculation about why Loukas Christofides, Greek shipping tycoon, had divorced his wife so abruptly and denied her custody of their daughter. 'It must have made some interesting reading,' she managed.

'No, it didn't, actually.'

She stared at him in confusion. 'What do you mean?'

'I didn't read it.'

'Why…why not?'

'Because even now I believe we shared something on that island, something important and different. I don't know why you ran from me, but I want to understand.' He stopped, his chest heaving, his gaze blazing into hers. 'Help me understand, Grace.'

How could she refuse when he asked her so rawly? And maybe…maybe he did understand. He *could.* She swallowed, her heart beating so hard it hurt. 'It's a long story,' she whispered.

'I have all the time in the world.' He sat down on her sofa, his body seeming relaxed although she still felt his tension. 'Why did you say I might hate you?' he asked quietly when the silence had ticked on for several minutes.

Grace knew he'd painted her as a victim, the most innocent of portraits. Now she would have to tell him the truth, in bold, stark colours. He would know, and he might leave here hating her more than ever before.

Or he might understand, forgive and love you more than ever before.

Did she dare hope?

Swallowing, she sat down across from him, her hands tucked between her knees. 'I've told you a bit about my marriage. About Loukas.'

'A little,' Khalis agreed neutrally. She hadn't said anything yet, and still it was so hard. Every explanation felt like an excuse.

'And that our marriage was troubled.'

'Yes, I'm aware of that, Grace.'

'I know.' She closed her eyes. He knew a little of how unhappy she'd been, trapped on that wretched island. Yet to go into detail now, to try to explain how desperate and lonely and scared she'd felt—wouldn't it all just sound as if she were justifying her actions? Khalis would certainly think so. He had given himself no excuses for accepting his father's help even after he'd realised the extent of his corruption. She wouldn't give herself any, either.

'Grace,' he prompted, and impatience edged his voice. Grace sighed and opened her eyes. There was, she knew, only one way to tell him the truth. Without any explanations, reasons or excuses. Just the stark, sordid facts. And see what he did with them.

'You've probably wondered how Loukas managed to gain complete custody of Katerina.'

'I assumed he worked the system, bribed a judge.' He paused, his voice carefully even. 'You implied as much.'

'Yes, but there was more to it than that. The truth is, he painted me as an unfit mother.' She gestured to the packet of papers he'd thrown onto her table. 'If you'd read those articles, you'd see. He made me seem completely irresponsible, negligent—' She swallowed and forced herself to go on. 'By the time he'd finished, anyone would think I hadn't cared about my daughter at all.'

Khalis's gaze remained steady on hers. 'But they would be wrong, wouldn't they?'

'They'd be wrong in thinking I didn't care,' Grace said in a low voice, brushing impatiently at the corners of her eyes. 'But they wouldn't be wrong in thinking I'd been negligent.' She drew in a shuddering breath. 'I was.'

Khalis said nothing for a moment. Grace forced herself to hold his gaze, but she couldn't tell a thing from his shuttered eyes, his expressionless face. The tears that had threatened were gone now, replaced with a deep and bone-weary resignation.

'Negligent,' he finally repeated. 'How?'

Again Grace hesitated. She wanted to rush to her own defence, to explain she'd never meant to be negligent, she'd never actually put Katerina in danger—but what was the point? The fact remained that she had betrayed her husband. Her family. Herself. She took a breath, let it out slowly. 'I had an affair.'

All Khalis did was blink, but Grace still felt his recoil. He was surprised, of course. Shocked. He'd been expecting something sympathetic, something perhaps about post-partum depression or her abusive husband or who knew what. All along he'd been thinking that she'd been hurt, not that she'd done the hurting. Not an affair. Not a sordid, sexual, adulterous affair.

'An affair,' he said without any expression at all.

'Yes,' she confirmed, tonelessly now. 'With the man who managed the island property. Gardening, house repairs—'

'I don't care what he *did*.'

'I know. I just…' She shook her head. 'I told you I didn't want to tell you,' she said in a low voice.

Khalis didn't speak, and neither did Grace. The silence that yawned between them now was worse than any words could have been. Finally he asked, 'And while you had this affair…you were negligent of your daughter?'

'I never put her in danger or anything like that,' she whispered. 'I loved her. I still love her.' Her voice wavered and she strove for control. Khalis needed to hear the facts without tears or sentiment. 'That whole time is a blur. I was so unhappy—I didn't knowingly neglect her, of course not. I just…I just wasn't the mother I wanted to be.'

'Or the wife, apparently.'

His cool observation was like a dagger thrust straight to the heart. Grace blinked hard. 'I know what it sounds like. Maybe it's a blur because I don't want to remember.' Yet she'd never been able to truly forget. How could you not remember and not forget at the same time? More contradictions. 'I'm not trying to make excuses,' she said. 'How can I? I'm just trying to explain—'

'Why you had this affair.'

'How I don't really remember.'

Khalis let out a rush of breath that sounded almost like a laugh, yet without any humour in it at all. 'How convenient,' he said, 'for you not to remember.'

'I'm not lying, Khalis.'

'You virtually lied to me from the moment I met you—'

'That is *not* fair.' Her voice rose, surprising her. 'Why should I have told you such a thing when I barely knew you?' She stuck out her hand in a mockery of an introduction. 'Hello, my name is Grace Turner, I'm an art appraiser and an adulteress?'

Khalis rose from the sofa, prowling around the room with a restless, angry energy. 'There were plenty of times after that,' he said, his words almost a growl. 'When you knew how I felt about you—'

'I know—' she cut him off with a whisper '—I know. And I was afraid, I admit that. I didn't want you to look at me…the way you're looking at me now.' With his face

so terribly expressionless, as if he could not decide if she
were a stranger or someone he knew, never mind loved.

And she loved him. She'd fallen in love with him on
the island, with his tenderness and gentleness and understanding. She'd fallen in love with him despite that hardness inside him that she was seeing and feeling now. And
she didn't know if her love was enough. She said nothing,
simply waited for his verdict. Would he walk away from
her just as he had from his family, no second chances, no
regrets?

'How long?' he finally asked.

'How long…?'

'How long did you have this affair?'

She hesitated, the words drawn reluctantly from her.
'About six weeks.'

'And how long were you married?'

'Nearly two years.'

Khalis said nothing. Grace knew how awful it all
sounded. How could she, with a little baby and a new
husband, have gone and sought out another man? How
could she have deceived her husband and lost her daughter? What kind of woman did that?

She did. Had. And if she hadn't been able to forget or
forgive her actions, how could a man like Khalis?

Khalis stopped by the window, his back to her as he
stared out at the darkness. 'And I suppose,' he said in a
detached voice, 'your husband found out about the affair.
And was furious.'

'Yes. He didn't want anyone to know he'd been… That
I'd…' She stopped miserably. 'So in the courts he painted
me as a negligent mother instead.'

'But you weren't.'

His observation, even when delivered in such a cold

voice, gave her the thinnest thread of hope. 'I don't *think*...
I don't know what I was.'

Khalis didn't answer. His back was still to her. 'How?'
he finally asked.

Grace blinked. 'How...?'

'How did he find out?'

'Do you really need to know all these details?' she asked
rawly. 'How does it help anything—?'

'He walked in on you, didn't he?' Khalis said. He turned
around and Grace quelled at his icy expression. This was
the man who had faced down his father, who had walked
away from his family. 'On you and your lover.'

Her scorching blush, she knew, was all the answer he
needed. Khalis said nothing and Grace gazed blindly down
at her lap. She couldn't bear the look of condemnation she
knew she'd see on his face.

He let out a shuddering breath. 'I thought you'd been
abused,' he said quietly. 'Emotionally or physically—
something. Something terrible. I hated your ex-husband
for hurting you.'

Grace blinked hard, her gaze still on her lap. 'I know,'
she said softly.

'And all along...' He stopped and then, through her
blurred vision, from the corner of her eye, she saw him
pick up his coat.

Her throat was so tight she could barely choke out the
words. 'I'm sorry.'

The only answer was the click of the door as Khalis
shut it behind him.

CHAPTER TEN

'You look,' Michel told Grace a week later, 'like a plate of warmed-up rice pudding.'

'That doesn't sound very attractive.' She closed the door to her employer's office, eyebrows raised. 'You wanted to see me?'

Michel stared at her hard. 'I mean it, Grace. You look terrible.'

'Clearly you're full of compliments today.'

He sighed and moved around to his desk. Grace waited, trying to keep her expression enquiring and friendly even as her body tensed and another headache began its relentless pounding. This last week had been horrible. She had not seen or heard from Khalis since he'd walked out of her apartment without a word, leaving her too empty and aching even to cry. She'd drifted through the days, feeling numb and yet possessing a terrible awareness of what lay beneath that nothingness—an awful, yawning expanse of grief and despair. Just knowing it was there, like the deep and frigid waters beneath a thin layer of black ice, kept her awake at night, staring into the darkness, memories dancing through her mind like ghosts.

Memories of her marriage, the deep unhappiness she'd felt, the terrible mistakes she'd made. Memories of holding Katerina for the first time, the joy so deep it almost felt like pain as she'd kissed her wrinkled, downy head. Memories of the court hearing that had left her as close to longing for death as she'd ever been.

Memories of Khalis.

She'd taken her one night knowing she would only have the memories to sustain her, but they did not. They tormented her with their tenderness and sweetness, and she lay in bed with her eyes closed, imagining she could feel his arms around her, his body pressed against her, his thumb brushing the tear from her cheek.

Sometimes sleep came, and always dawn, and she stumbled through another day alone.

'Is there something you wanted?' Grace asked, keeping her smile in place with effort. Michel sighed and steepled his fingers under his chin.

'Not precisely. Khalis Tannous has donated the last two works in his father's collection.'

'The Leonardos?'

'Yes.'

Grace affected a look of merely professional interest. She had no idea if she succeeded or not. 'And where is he donating them?'

'The Fitzwilliam in Cambridge.'

The Fitzwilliam in Cambridge was practically a second home.

Grace angled her face away from Michel's narrowed gaze. 'A rather odd choice,' she said.

'Is it? I thought it quite spectacularly appropriate.'

'What do you mean?'

'Come now, Grace. It's quite obvious to anyone with eyes in his head that something happened between you and Tannous on that island.'

'I see,' Grace said after a second's pause.

'And that it made you more miserable than ever,' Michel

continued. 'I had hopes that Tannous might bring you back to life—'

'I wasn't *dead*,' Grace interjected and Michel gave her a mirthless smile.

'As good as. I'm your employer, Grace, but I've also known you since you were a child, and I care about you. I never liked seeing you so unhappy, and I like it even less now. I thought Tannous might help you—'

'Is that why you insisted I go to that island?'

Michel gave a dismissive and completely Gallic shrug. 'I sent you there because you are my best appraiser of Renaissance art. But I must confess I don't like the result.' He stared at her rather beadily from behind his desk. 'You're enough to make the Mona Lisa lose her smile.'

Grace thought of Leda's sorrowful half-smile and shook her head. 'I'm sorry. I'll try to—'

'Don't be *sorry*,' Michel cut her off impatiently. 'I didn't bring you in here to ask for an apology.'

'Then why?'

Michel was silent for a long moment. 'What did he do to you?' he finally asked.

'Nothing, Michel. He didn't do anything to me.' *Except make me fall in love with him.*

'Then why are you looking—?'

'Like a bowl of warmed-up rice pudding?' She gave him a small sad smile. 'Because he found out,' she said simply. 'He found out about me.'

Khalis gazed down at the financial report he was reading and tried to make sense of the numbers for the third time. In disgust at his own lack of focus, he pushed them away and stared out of the window of his father's office in Rome's EUR business district. Below him tourists and office workers bustled about their business, whether it was snapping photos or grabbing their lunch.

He should have forgotten her by now. Or at least stopped thinking of her. He'd been able to do that for his own family; why couldn't he do the same for a slip of a woman who had virtually lied to him and betrayed her own marriage vows?

Instead he kept remembering everything about her. How her eyes had lightened with sudden humour and her lips had curved as if she wasn't used to smiling. Her passion and strength of purpose for her work, her focus which matched his own. The softness of her breasts pressed against his chest, her body so wonderfully yielding against his.

And how she had deceived and duped him into thinking she was innocent, a victim like Leda. She should have told him. At some point during their time together, she should have told him. No, he realised with sudden savagery, it wasn't the telling that mattered. It was the doing. He wanted her not to have had the affair at all. After such a huge betrayal…how could he trust her? *Love* her?

His intercom buzzed, disrupting his pointless recriminations. 'A phone call for you, Mr Tannous, on line one.'

'Who from?'

'He didn't say, sir. But he said it was urgent.'

Khalis felt a flicker of irritation. He paid a receptionist to field his calls, not just pass them on. 'Very well,' he said tersely and picked up his phone.

'Yes?'

'Hello, Khalis.'

Khalis's fingers froze around the phone as his mind blanked with shock even as he registered that familiar voice. A voice he hadn't heard in fifteen years. His brother.

His brother who was supposed to be dead. Khalis's

mind raced in circles. Was his father alive as well? What the hell had happened? Swallowing, he finally managed to speak.

'Ammar,' he said without expression. 'You're alive.'

His brother let out a dry, humourless laugh. 'You don't sound pleased I am back from the dead.'

'You died to me fifteen years ago.'

'I need to talk to you.'

Khalis fought down the tide of emotion hearing his brother's voice had caused to sweep over him. Shock, anger, pain, and both a joy and regret he didn't want to acknowledge. 'We have nothing to say to each other.'

'Please, Khalis,' he said, but it still sounded like a command, the older brother bullying him into submission once more, and his resolve hardened.

'No.'

'I've changed—'

'People don't change, Ammar. Not that much.' Khalis wondered distantly why he didn't just hang up.

'Do you really believe that?' Ammar asked quietly, and for the first time in Khalis's memory he sounded sad rather than angry.

'I...' *Did* he believe that? He'd been living that truth for the last fifteen years. His father wouldn't change. Couldn't. Because if he had...if he could...then maybe Khalis wouldn't have had to leave in the dramatic fashion that he did. Maybe he could have stayed, or returned, or worked something out. Maybe Jamilah wouldn't have died.

Khalis swallowed, forced the agonising thoughts back. 'Yes,' he said stonily. 'I do believe that.' And then, his hand trembling, he hung up the phone.

The ensuing silence seemed to reverberate through the room. Khalis stabbed at his intercom. 'Please block any calls from that number,' he told the receptionist, who bumbled through an apology before Khalis severed the connection. He rose from the desk and paced the office restlessly, feeling caged not by the four walls but by his thoughts. His memories.

Had Ammar changed? He'd changed once before. Khalis had a sudden sharp memory of when his brother had turned eight. Their father had called him out of the nursery where they'd been playing with Lego together, neither of them knowing it was to be the last day of boyish pleasures. Khalis didn't know what Balkri had said or done to his oldest son that day, but when Ammar returned his lip was bleeding and the light had gone out of his eyes. He never had a kind word or action for Khalis again.

As the years had passed the rivalry between them had hardened into something unforgiving and cruel. Ammar always had to win, and not just win but humiliate Khalis. He was older, stronger, tougher and he let his little brother know it at every opportunity. Grace had asked him if Ammar was a bully, but it hadn't been a simple case of sibling rivalry. Ammar had been driven by something darker, and sometimes Khalis thought he'd seen a torment of emotion in his brother's eyes he knew he didn't understand. If he tried to, Ammar just turned away or hit him. There was no going back to those simple days of childhood. There was no going back at all.

Do people change?

Ammar might not have changed, but could he make that kind of assumption about everyone? About Grace?

Khalis halted his restless prowling and stared unseeingly out of the office window. He pictured Grace as he'd last seen her, her head bowed in regret, tears starting in her eyes. Did he believe she'd changed, or was he going to freeze her in her weakest moment, refuse to allow her to move past it? How much was his experience of his father and brother colouring his perception of Grace?

She was different, he realised with a shaft of self-recrimination. Of course she was. He still didn't like the stark reality of it, he knew. He wished things could be different. But he'd told Grace there was no point in looking back, no point in useless regrets. He wanted to look forward.

He turned away from the window, a new resolve hardening inside him. He needed to see Grace again. Speak to her. *Help me understand*, he'd asked. But he hadn't understood, not then. Maybe they both needed a second chance.

Grace straightened her simple grey sheath dress and glanced round the crowd of art enthusiasts and academics that comprised the guest list for tonight's reception at the Fitzwilliam Museum. Khalis was once again being hailed a hero for donating his father's works of art, in this case the two Leonardos of Leda.

'You must be thrilled,' one of her old professors told her as she plucked a glass of champagne from one of the circulating trays. 'Such important works of art being exhibited so close to home!'

'Yes, it's wonderful news for the museum,' Grace answered dutifully. Cambridge didn't really feel like home although she did still possess the house on Grange Road where she'd grown up. She let it out to visiting academics. And as for Khalis donating the works to the Fitzwilliam... *why* had he done that? Grace had wrestled with that question for many sleepless nights. It almost seemed like the kind of tender, thoughtful gesture that had made her fall in love with him—but he hated her now. So what kind of message was he trying to send?

She continued her progression around the grand entrance hall of the museum, chatting to guests, keeping an eye on the door. Even though she knew there was no real point, she still could not keep herself from looking for him and wanting to know when he was here.

Even if she hadn't felt it—that curious prickling between her shoulder blades—she would have known he'd arrived by the speculative murmurs that rippled through the crowd. Tall, imposing in an immaculate navy suit and utterly gorgeous, Khalis would draw admiration wherever he went. Grace stepped back against the wall, holding her untouched glass of champagne in front of her like some kind of shield. She saw Khalis's grey-green gaze search the crowd and knew he was looking for her. And then he found her, his unwavering stare like a laser that pierced all of her defences. She stood there, still clutching her glass, unable to move or even think.

Khalis's face was neutral yet his eyes seemed to blaze right into her, searing her soul. He really did hate her. With effort Grace turned away, walked on wobbly legs towards the next knot of people and tried desperately to seem unconcerned as their chatter washed over her in an incomprehensible wave.

Regret lashed him as Khalis watched Grace walk away. Her back was straight, her figure lithe and slender in the simple silk sheath she wore. Had she lost weight? Her face had been so pale, her eyes huge as they'd gazed at each other.

He'd had plenty of time to acknowledge how his past had coloured his perception of the present, of Grace. He'd duped himself, just as he had with his own father. He'd wanted to believe only the best of her and so he'd refused to heed her warnings, insisted on painting his own rosy picture.

And when she'd finally worked up the courage to give him the truth, he'd walked away. He'd wanted her trust—demanded it, even—only to abuse it at the first opportunity.

Why, he wondered bleakly, should she ever trust him again?

CHAPTER ELEVEN

GRACE felt her nerves tauten throughout the evening, so by the time the reception came to an end she felt as if they were overstretched threads, ready to snap. Her body ached with the effort of appearing interested and unconcerned, as well as thrilled that Khalis had donated such magnificent works of art to the museum.

Khalis, she'd observed, had circulated around the room in distinct counterpoint to her rotation; there could be no question he was avoiding her—or at least that she was avoiding him. Perhaps he was simply indifferent to her now. Yet, despite the distance between them, she remained constantly and agonisingly aware of him. Even as she chatted with guests she strained to hear his low, husky voice, felt every one of his easy movements reverberate through her own body.

At least she wouldn't see him again. The Leonardos had been the last two works from the Tannous collection. There would be no more receptions or galas, no need to encounter him at all. No risk, no danger. The thought should have brought blessed relief, not the wave of devastation Grace felt instead.

Finally the guests were trickling out into Trumpington Street and Grace found an opportunity to slip away. Khalis, she'd seen, was still chatting with a few hangers-on. She hurried out of the entrance hall, grabbing her coat, and into the damp night. It was midsummer, but the weather was wet and chilly and she wrapped her coat more firmly around herself as she headed down the street, her heels clicking on the slick pavement.

So that was that, she thought dully as she walked towards the hotel in the centre of town where she'd booked a room for the night. She'd probably never see him again. Talk to him again. *Touch* him again…

'Grace.'

For a second Grace thought she must be imagining things. Fantasising that she'd heard Khalis because she missed him so much, even though she knew she shouldn't—

'Grace.'

Slowly, stunned, she turned around. Khalis stood there, his hair damp and spiky with rain. He'd forgotten his coat.

Grace simply stared, her mind empty of thoughts. Why had he sought her out? He didn't look as if he was angry but she could not think of a single reason why he would come and find her. Surely everything had been said that awful night at her apartment?

'Are you staying at your father's house?' he finally asked after they'd simply stared at each other for an endless moment.

Grace shook her head. 'I've let it out. I booked into a hotel, just for the one night.'

'Tomorrow you go back to Paris?'

She nodded. 'Thank you for donating the Leonardos to the Fitzwilliam,' she said awkwardly. 'The museum is thrilled, of course.'

'Well,' Khalis answered with a crooked smile, 'the Louvre has the Mona Lisa, after all. And I know how much you care about these paintings. I thought they should go to your second home.'

Sudden tears stung Grace's eyes as she slowly shook her head. 'Thank you,' she said. 'It was kind of you, especially considering—' Her throat closed up and all she could do was stare at him, knowing her heart was in her eyes. Her heartbreak.

'Oh, Grace.'

In one fluid movement Khalis strode forward and pulled her into his arms, wrapping her in a gentle yet fierce hug. Grace felt the damp wool of his suit against her cheek, her mind frozen on the fact that he was here, hugging her, and it felt unbelievably, unbearably wonderful.

With effort she pulled away. 'Someone will see—'

'To hell with that.'

'I don't understand you,' Grace whispered. 'Why are you here? Why are you—?' *Hugging me. Looking at me as if... Almost as if you love me.*

'Because I'm sorry, Grace. I messed up. A lot.' His voice wavered on the last word and she stared.

'*You* messed up?'

'I shouldn't have walked out on you. I was shocked, I admit that, but I…I wanted you to trust me and then I threw that trust away with both hands.'

She blinked, taking in his words, the self-recrimination that lanced each one. 'You judge yourself pretty harshly.'

'I had no right to judge you.'

'I know what I did, Khalis—'

'I know you do. Everything you said and did is marked by guilt, Grace. I couldn't believe I didn't see that before.'

She angled her face away from him, knowing he was right. Wishing he wasn't. 'I don't know how to let go of it,' she whispered.

'I asked you to help me understand,' Khalis said quietly. 'And you told me the truth, but I don't think you told me all of it.'

She nearly choked. 'What more do you want me to say—?'

'Help me understand,' Khalis said as he drew her to him, his arms enfolding her and holding her close. Accepting her, even now. Especially now. 'Not just the things you regret or wish were different. Help me understand *you*.'

'I don't know how—'

'Tell me. Tell me everything.'

It wasn't until she was lying in his arms that she started to speak. Khalis knew he had to be patient. Gentler than he ever had been before. He'd thought it had been hard to get her to trust him before, when she hadn't told him anything and he'd thought she was perfect. Now he knew there were things he wouldn't want to hear, facts he would be reluctant to accept. And still he needed to hold her close and justify this fragile trust she'd placed in him.

She stirred, her hair brushing against his bare chest. He'd brought her to the luxury hotel he'd booked in town, the windows of the penthouse suite overlooking the River Cam. She'd come into the room warily, her eyes wide as she took in the huge four-poster bed piled high with pillows and a silken duvet.

He'd been about to reassure her that they could just talk, that all he wanted was to talk—well, sort of. After nearly three months apart, he wanted *her* desperately.

'Grace—' he began, and then she turned to him suddenly and wrapped her arms around him. He pulled her close, buried his face in her hair, inhaling its sweet fragrance.

'I missed you,' she said in a whisper. 'I missed me with you.' And he knew what she meant. He'd missed her, too, missed the sense of rightness he felt when he was with her. He kissed her then and, though he meant to keep it gentle, neither of them could control the tide of desire that swept over them as their lips met and met again. They'd missed each other too much to go slowly. In one fluid movement Khalis undid the zip of Grace's dress and she wriggled out of it, laughing a little as it snagged round her ankles.

'Another dress bites the dust,' Khalis said with a grin as he tossed it aside. Grace kicked off her heels. He pulled her towards the bed, his breathing turned harsh and ragged as they both fell upon its softness and each other, hands roving over skin with an urgent need to remember, to feel, to know.

Grace arched upwards as Khalis slid his hand between her thighs, his own voice coming out in a moan of longing. 'Oh, Grace. I missed this. I missed you.'

'Yes,' she panted, her head thrown back, her fingers digging into his shoulders as she urged him closer. And then he was filling her, making her gasp and his heart fill with the wonder of it, with the knowledge that the connection they'd both experienced was finally, joyously restored.

Afterwards she lay in his arms, her heart thundering against his as he brushed her dry cheek. 'No tears,' he said softly, his hand cupping her face, and she smiled against his palm.

'No tears,' she answered, and then neither of them spoke for a long moment. The weight of the words she hadn't said lay between them, but as Khalis held her he knew they bore it together. And then she stirred, settled herself against him and began.

'I first met Loukas when I was just fourteen,' she said softly. She ran her hand down his arms, her fingers curling around his bicep, holding onto him like an anchor. Khalis pulled her closer and waited. 'My mother had died the year before and I suppose I was lonely. My father was wonderful, but he was also easily distracted, absorbed by his books. And Loukas was so kind then. He was full of important plans about how he'd make his fortune, but he still made time for me.' She sighed and her hair whispered against his chest once more. 'The next time I saw him was at my father's funeral. I was twenty-six, and I'd just finished my doctorate. I was about to join an auction house in London, and before he died I felt like I had everything before me. But then...' She paused, shaking her head. 'I felt so alone. I realised I had no one left, and when Loukas invited me out, listened to me...well, it felt wonderful. I hadn't had any really serious relationships; I'd been too involved in my studies. And at that moment...' She paused. 'Sometimes I wonder if we'd met at a different point, if I would have noticed him at all. Maybe that's just...wishful thinking, I don't know. I don't think my head would have been quite so turned.'

'You were vulnerable.'

She shook her head. 'That's just an excuse.'

'We're not talking about excuses,' Khalis reminded her. 'Just understanding.'

'We were married within six weeks. It was far too fast, I see that now. I barely knew what I was doing. I was still grieving, really. I still thought of him as the university student with a kind word for me and a friendly smile, but he'd changed. He was wealthy now, terribly wealthy, and I think...I think he saw me as a possession. A prized one, but...' She stopped, swallowing, before she continued in a voice heavy with remembrance. 'He took me to his island for what I thought was a honeymoon. I thought we'd go back, live in London, have a normal life.' She stopped again, and he felt her body tense. He ran his hand down her shoulder and arm, pulled her closer to him. 'He left

me there,' Grace confessed in a whisper. 'He informed
the auction house that I wasn't taking up the post, and told
me he wanted to keep me safe. He made it sound like he
was trying to take care of me, but I felt—' She drew in a
ragged breath. 'I felt like Leda, trapped in that little room
with no one to see her or even know she was there.' She
gave something that Khalis supposed was meant to be a
laugh, but it wobbled too much. 'It sounds so ridiculous
because I wasn't really a prisoner. I mean, I was a grown
woman—I could have arranged transport or something. I
wasn't *trapped.*'

'But?' Khalis prompted when it seemed as if she
wouldn't go on.

'But I was afraid. Loukas felt like the only person I
had in the world and, even though he wasn't there most of
the time, I didn't want to lose him. And sometimes I convinced myself that it was all reasonable, that living on an
island paradise was no hardship.'

'No wonder you hated Alhaja with all of its security
and walls.'

'I don't like feeling trapped. Or managed. Loukas was
always telling me what to do, even what to think.' She
sighed, shaking her head. 'I think I was working up the
courage to leave when I found out I was pregnant. I knew
I couldn't leave him then. He wouldn't let me, and I still
wanted our family to work.' She rolled over to face him
now, her eyes clouded with sadness and yet so heartbreakingly clear. She hid nothing from him now. 'After Katerina
was born, I thought it would be enough. It should have
been enough. But she didn't sleep or nurse well and I was
tired. Loukas had hired a nanny to help me but she was
awful, as bossy and controlling as he was. At times I felt
like I was going out of my mind.'

Khalis said nothing, just kept stroking her back, her shoulder, her arm. Touches to show he was listening. He understood. 'And then,' she whispered and stopped. She rolled back onto her side, tucked her knees up into her chest. The silence ticked on. 'Loukas hired him, you know,' she whispered. 'To tend the property. Sometimes I wonder... I think maybe...maybe he was testing me, and I failed.'

'That's not how a marriage is meant to work.'

'No,' Grace said after a moment, her voice no more than a scratch of sound. 'None of it was meant to work that way.' Her shoulders shook then and he knew she was crying, not just tears trickling down her face, but sobs that wrenched her whole body.

Khalis didn't say anything. He just held her, rubbing her back, his cheek pressed against her hair. The sound of her sorrow made his own eyes sting. How could he have ever doubted this woman? Thought he couldn't love her?

He loved her now more than ever.

Finally her sobs abated and she gave a loud sniff, a trembling laugh. 'I'm sorry. I haven't cried like that since... well, since forever.'

'I thought as much.'

She rolled over to face him again. Her eyes were red and puffy from weeping, her face completely blotchy. Khalis smiled and pressed a gentle kiss to her lips.

'You're beautiful,' he told her. 'And I love you.'

Her mouth curved in a trembling smile. 'I love you, too.' She laid her palm against his cheek. 'You know,' she said softly, 'for the first time I feel like the past isn't hanging over me. Suffocating me. I almost feel...free.' She stroked his cheek and another tear slid down her cheek. 'Thank you,' she whispered.

* * *

When Grace awoke the bed was empty and sunlight flooded the room. She lay there, the memories of last night washing over her in a healing tide. She never would have thought telling Khalis everything would feel so good, so restorative. Surely there were no secrets between them now.

What about your daughter?

Grace rolled over onto her side. Loukas would have found out about last night. Somehow, some way, he would know she'd been indiscreet. And even as her heart ached at this knowledge, she realised she no longer lived in the kind of terror he'd kept her in for four long years. With Khalis's help, she could fight the custody arrangement. She didn't know how long it would take or how they would do it, but for the first time in four years she had hope. It was as powerful and heady a feeling as the love she felt for Khalis. Smiling, she rose from the bed. She heard the sound of the shower from the bathroom and saw a tray with a carafe of coffee, a couple of cups and a newspaper. She poured herself a cup and reached for the paper.

Ammar Tannous survives helicopter crash.

It wasn't even on the front page, just a corner of the second page, hardly noticeable, and yet the words seemed to jump out and grab her by the throat. Khalis's brother was alive.

She'd barely processed this information when the bathroom door opened and Khalis emerged, dressed only in boxers, a towel draped over his shoulders.

'Good morning.'

She looked up, the paper still in her hands. 'Khalis… Khalis, I've just read…'

'Something amazing, it would seem.' He smiled as he reached for the carafe of coffee.

'Look at this.' She thrust the paper at him, pointing to the article about Ammar. And in the second it took Khalis to read the headline, his mouth compressing, she felt her hope and joy being doused by the icy chill of foreboding.

He glanced away from the paper and finished pouring his coffee. 'What about it?'

'*What about it?* Khalis, that's your brother. Isn't it?' For a second she thought she must have got it wrong. Surely he couldn't be so cold about *this*.

'It appears to be.' He sat across from her and sipped his coffee. Grace would have thought he was completely indifferent except for the tension radiating from his body. The bone china cup looked as if it might snap between his fingers. 'I went to file a custody appeal this morning.'

Grace blinked, trying to keep up. 'A custody—'

'My legal team thinks the trial judge abused his wide discretion,' Khalis explained. 'And because there was so little finding to support the court order, it's manifestly in error. I think you could have complete custody.'

Even as that thought caused new hope to leap within her, Grace shook her head. 'You're just changing the subject.'

'I'm talking about your daughter.'

'And I'm talking about your brother. You don't even seem surprised that he's alive.' She saw a wariness enter his eyes, felt his hesitation. 'You knew, didn't you?' she said slowly. 'You already knew.'

Khalis glanced away. 'He phoned me a few days ago.'

'And what…what did he say?'

'I didn't really talk to him.'

'Why not?'

He snapped his gaze back to her. 'Because he was up to

his neck in the same illegal activities as my father. I don't trust him, don't even know him any more. As far as I'm concerned, he's my enemy.'

She stared at him, saw the taut, angry energy of his body, and knew there was more to this than Khalis was saying. More darkness and pain and fear. He'd helped her look into the abyss of her own past regrets and mistakes last night; maybe it was her turn to help him.

'Couldn't you at least talk to him?' she asked.

'I don't see any point.'

'Maybe he's changed—'

Khalis gave a short, hard laugh. 'He suggested the same thing. People don't change, Grace. Not that much.'

She felt a sudden shaft of pain pierce her. 'Don't they?'

Khalis glanced at her, his lips pressed in a thin line. 'You know I didn't mean you.'

'I don't really see the difference.'

'You don't see the difference between you and my brother? Come on, Grace.'

'What *is* the difference, Khalis? It sounds like we're two people who made mistakes and regret them.'

'You think Ammar regrets—'

'You said he told you he'd changed.'

Khalis looked away. 'This is ridiculous. You made one single mistake which you regret bitterly, and Ammar made dozens—'

Grace felt herself go cold. 'Oh, I see,' she said. 'There's a maximum on how many mistakes you can make? I'm all right because I just made the one?'

'You're twisting my words.'

'I don't understand why you can't just talk to him at least.'

'Because I don't *want* to,' Khalis snapped. Colour

slashed his cheekbones. He looked angry, Grace thought, but he also looked afraid.

'You don't *want* to forgive him,' she said slowly. 'Do you?' Khalis didn't answer, but she saw the truth in his eyes. 'Why not?' she asked, her voice soft with sorrow. 'Why do you want to hold onto all that anger and pain? I know how it can cripple you—'

'You *don't* know,' Khalis said shortly. He rose from the table and moved to the window, his back to her. 'I don't want to talk about this any more.'

'So I'm meant to tell you everything,' she said, her voice rising. 'I'm meant to completely open my heart and soul but you get to have certain parts of your life be off-limits. Well, *that* seems fair.'

The very air seemed to shiver with the sudden suppressed tension, tension Grace hadn't even really known existed between them. She'd thought they'd both been laid bare and healed last night, but only she had. Khalis was still living in the torment of his past, holding onto his hard heart. How could she not have seen that? She'd seen that unyielding iron core the very first day they'd met. It didn't just magically melt or disappear. She'd been dreaming of happy endings, but now she saw that as long as Khalis held onto this anger they were just fairy tales.

'Khalis,' she said quietly, 'if you aren't willing to forgive your brother, if you can't believe that he might have changed, how can I believe you think I have?'

Khalis let out a ragged breath. 'It's completely different—'

'No, it isn't. It really isn't.' She shook her head sadly. She wanted to help him, but she didn't know if she could. If he'd let her. 'I almost wish it was. But don't you see how this—this coldness in you will affect anything we have together?'

He turned back to her, his eyes flashing a warning. 'You don't know my family, Grace.'

'Then tell me. Tell me what they did that's so bad you can't give your brother—your brother whom you thought was dead—a second chance.'

Khalis swung away from her and raked a hand through his hair. 'You are trying to equate two very different situations. And it simply doesn't work.'

'But the principles are the same.' Grace rose and took a step closer to him. 'The heart involved in the relationships is the same—yours.'

Khalis let out a sound that was close to a laugh, but filled with disbelief and disgust. 'Are you saying I can't love you if I don't forgive my brother?'

Grace hesitated. She didn't want to make ultimatums or force Khalis to do something he wasn't ready for or capable of. Yet she also knew that they could have no real, secure future as long as he harboured this coldness towards his family. 'Ever since we first met,' she began, choosing her words with care, 'I sensed a darkness—a hardness in you that scares me.'

He turned around, eyebrows arched in cynical incredulity. 'I *scared* you? I thought you loved me.'

'I do, Khalis. That's why I'm saying this.'

'Cruel to be kind?' he jeered, and Grace knew she was getting closer to the heart of it. The heart of him, and the thing—whatever it was—he was afraid of.

'I'm not trying to be cruel,' she said. 'But I don't understand, Khalis. Why won't you even talk to your brother? Why do you refuse to mourn or even think of your family? Why are you so determined never to look back?'

'I told you, the past is past—'

'But it *isn't*—' Grace cut him off '—as long as it controls your actions.'

He stared at her long and hard and she ached to cross the room and hold him in her arms. 'You helped me face my demons,' she said softly. 'Maybe now you need to face yours.'

His features twisted and, with a lurch of mingled hope and sorrow, Grace thought she'd won. *They* had. Then he turned away and said tonelessly, 'That's just a lot of psychobabble.'

Her eyes stung. 'Do you really believe that?'

'Don't make this into something it isn't, Grace. This isn't about us. We can be perfectly happy without me ever seeing my brother again.'

'No. We can't.' Her words fell slowly into the stillness, as if from a great height. Grace imagined she could almost see the irrevocable ripples they created, like pebbles in a pond, disturbing the calm surface for ever.

He turned back to face her, shock replacing anger. 'What are you saying?'

'I'm saying,' Grace said, each word a knife-twist in her heart, 'that if you can't even talk to your brother—your brother whom you thought was dead—then I can't be with you.' He looked as if she'd just punched him. Maybe she had. 'I'm not trying to give you some kind of ultimatum—'

'Really?' he practically snarled. 'Because it looks that way from here.'

'I'm just stating facts, Khalis. Our relationship has been a mess of contradictions from the beginning. Keeping secrets even as we had this incredible connection. Amazing intimacy and terrible pain. Well, I don't want a relationship—a love—that is a contradiction. I want the real thing. Whole. Pure. Good. I want that with you.'

He let out a shuddering breath. 'When we first met, I put you on a pedestal. I thought you were perfect, and I was disappointed when you showed me your feet of clay.

But I accepted you, Grace. I accepted you and loved you just as you are. Yet now you can't do the same for me? I've got to be perfect?'

'No, Khalis.' She shook her head, blinked back tears. 'I don't want you to be perfect. I just want you to try.'

His mouth curved in a disbelieving and humourless smile. 'Try to be perfect.'

'No,' she said, her heart breaking now, 'just try to forgive.'

Khalis didn't answer, and that was answer enough. He couldn't do it, she realised. He couldn't even try to let go. And they couldn't have a future together—a secure, trusting future—as long as he didn't.

Slowly Grace walked over to the bed, where her clothes from last night still lay discarded on the floor. She reached for her dress. 'I think,' she said, 'I have a flight to catch.'

Khalis stared at the nondescript door of the hotel room where his brother was staying. It had taken two days to work up the courage to call Ammar, and then fly to Tunis where he was staying. Now he was here, standing in the hallway of a nameless hotel, the cries and clangs from the busy medina of metalwork and craft shops audible on the hot, dusty air.

Even now he was tempted to walk away. Grace had demanded answers, yet how could he explain his reasoning for refusing simply to speak to his brother? What kind of man could be so hard-hearted?

Apparently he could.

Yet the feeling—the *need*—to keep himself distant from his family was so instinctive it felt like a knee-jerk reflex. And when he'd heard Ammar's voice on the telephone, sounding so ragged and even broken, that deep-seated instinct had only grown stronger. Grace was right. He didn't want to forgive Ammar. He was afraid of what might happen if he did.

It had taken her leaving him—*devastating* him—for him to finally face his brother. His past.

Khalis raised one trembling fist and knocked on the door. He heard footsteps, and then the door opened and he was staring at his brother. Ammar still stood tall and imposing, reminding Khalis that his brother had always been older, stronger, tougher. Ammar's face looked gaunt, though, and there was a long scar snaking down the side of his face. He stared long and hard at Khalis, and then he stepped aside to let him in.

Khalis walked in slowly, his body almost vibrating with tension. The last time he'd seen Ammar he'd been twenty-one years old and leaving Alhaja. Ammar had laughed. *Good riddance*, he'd called. And then he'd turned away as if he couldn't care less.

'Thank you for coming,' Ammar said. He sounded the same, surly and impatient. Maybe he hadn't changed after all. Khalis realised he would be glad, and felt a spurt of shame.

'I'm not sure why I did,' Khalis answered. He couldn't manage any more. Raw emotion had grabbed him by the throat and had him in a stranglehold, making further speech impossible. He hadn't seen his brother in fifteen years. Hadn't spoken to him or even looked at a photograph of him. Hadn't *thought* of him, because to think of Ammar was to remember the happy days of their childhood, when they had been friends and comrades-in-arms. Not competitors. Not enemies.

To think of Ammar, Khalis knew with a sudden flash of pain, was to think of Jamilah and to regret. To wonder if he might have made a mistake in leaving all those years ago. And that was a thought he could not bear to consider for a moment.

'So,' he finally said, and his voice sounded rusty, 'you're alive.' As far as observations went, it was asinine. Yet Khalis felt robbed of intelligent thought as well as speech. Part of him wanted to reach forward and hug the brother he'd lost so long ago. The other part—the greater part, perhaps—still had a heart like a stone.

The heart involved in the relationships is the same—yours.

And he wanted that heart to belong to Grace. For her—for them—he had to try. 'Why did you want to talk to me?' he asked.

Ammar's face twisted in a grimace. 'You're my brother.'

'I haven't been your brother for fifteen years.'

'You'll always be my brother, Khalis.'

'What are you saying?' Khalis tried to keep his voice even. It was hard with so many contrary emotions running through him. Hope and fear. Anger and joy. *I don't want a relationship...that is a contradiction.* He swallowed. He had to see this through.

Ammar released a shuddering breath. 'God knows I have made many mistakes in this life, even as a boy. But I've changed—'

Khalis let out a disbelieving laugh, the sound harsh and cold. Grace was right. There was a coldness inside him, a hard darkness he did not know how to dispel. *She only wanted you to try.* 'How have you changed?' he managed.

'The helicopter crash—'

'A brush with death made you realise the error of your ways?' Khalis heard the sneer in his own voice.

'Something like that.' He gazed levelly at Khalis. 'Do you want to know what happened?'

He shrugged. 'Very well.'

'The engine failed. I think it was a genuine accident, although God knows our father always suspected some-one of trying to kill him.'

'When you deal with the dregs of society, that tends to happen.'

'I know,' Ammar said quietly.

Khalis gave another hard laugh. 'As well you should.'

'I was piloting the helicopter,' Ammar continued. 'When we realised we were going to crash, Father gave the one parachute to me.'

For a second Khalis was stunned into silence. He had not thought his father capable of any generosity of spirit. 'Why was there only one parachute?' he asked after a moment.

Ammar shrugged. 'Who knows? Maybe the old man only wanted there to be one so he could be sure to take it in case of an accident. I always thought he'd be the last one standing.'

'But he changed his mind?'

'He *changed*,' Ammar said quietly, and Khalis heard a note of sorrow in his brother's usually strident voice. 'He was dying. He'd been diagnosed with terminal cancer six months ago. It made him start to really think about things.'

'*Think* about things?'

'I know he had a lot to answer for. I think that's why he decided to hand the company over to you. He only did that a month or so before he died, you know. He talked about you, said he regretted being so harsh with you.' Ammar gave him a bleak smile. 'Admired what you'd done with yourself.'

It seemed so hard to believe. Painful to believe. The last time he'd seen his father, Balkri Tannous had spat in his face. Tried to hit him. And recklessly Khalis had told him he was taking Jamilah with him.

Over my dead body, Balkri Tannous had said. Except in the end it had been Jamilah's.

And still Khalis had left. Without her.

Pain stabbed at him, both at his head and his heart. This was why he never thought about the past. This was why he'd cut himself off from his family so utterly, had insisted his father or brother could not be redeemed. So he wouldn't wonder if he should have stayed. Or returned sooner. Or taken her anyway. Anything to have kept his sister alive.

'You're thinking of Jamilah,' Ammar said quietly and Khalis swung away, braced one hand against the door. He wanted to leave. He was *desperate* to leave, and yet the thought of Grace—the warmth of her smile, the *strength* of her—made him stay. 'It was an accident, you know,' Ammar said. 'Her death. She didn't mean to kill herself.' He paused, and Khalis closed his eyes. 'I knew you'd wonder.'

'How do you know it was an accident?'

'She was determined, Khalis. Determined to live. She told me so.'

Khalis let out a strangled sound, choking off the cry of anguish that howled inside him. 'If I'd come back for her—'

'You could not have prevented an accident.'

'If I'd stayed—'

'You couldn't have stayed.'

His hand clenched into a fist. 'Maybe I should have,' he said in a low voice. 'Maybe if I'd stayed, I could have changed things for the better.'

His back to Ammar, Khalis didn't hear his brother move. He just felt his hand heavy on his shoulder. 'Khalis, it took an act of God and my own father's death for me to want to change. It took Father's diagnosis for him to even think about changing. Do not attempt to carry the world on your shoulders. We were grown men. We were not your responsibility, and neither was Jamilah.'

Khalis didn't speak for a long moment. He couldn't. 'So what happened next?' he finally asked.

'I parachuted into the sea and managed to get to land. A small island south of here, closer to the coast. It had fresh water, so I knew I could survive for a few days at least. I dislocated my shoulder when I landed, but I managed to fix it.' Ammar spoke neutrally enough, but Khalis was humbled anyway. He could not imagine enduring such a catastrophe.

'And?' he asked after a pause.

'After six days I managed to flag down a fishing boat, and they brought me to a small village on the coast of Tunisia. I'd developed a fever by that point and I was out of my mind for several days. By the time I knew who I was and I remembered everything, weeks had passed since the crash. I knew I needed to speak with you, so I flew to San Francisco to find out where you were, and then to Rome.'

'How did you even know about my company?'

'I've kept track of what you've been doing,' Ammar said. 'All along.'

And meanwhile Khalis had deliberately refused to read or listen to anything about Tannous Enterprises. Again he felt that hot rush of guilt. He couldn't bear the thought of his brother or father regretting his departure, watching him from afar. He couldn't bear the thought he'd been wrong.

'I know I wasn't a good brother to you,' Ammar said.

Khalis just shrugged. 'Sibling rivalry.'

'It was worse than that.' He didn't answer. He knew it was. 'Please forgive me, Khalis.'

Ammar couldn't say it plainer than that. Khalis registered the heartfelt sincerity in his brother's gaunt face, and said nothing. The words he knew his brother wanted to hear stuck in his throat.

If I forgive you then the past can't be the past any more and I'll have to live with the guilt and regret of knowing I should have stayed and saved Jamilah. And I don't think I can survive that. I'm not strong enough.

But Grace was strong. Grace made him strong. And he knew, just as Grace had known, it wasn't only Ammar he needed to forgive. It was himself.

You helped me face my demons. Maybe now you need to face yours.

His throat worked. His eyes stung. And somehow he found the words, raw and rusty, scraping his throat and tearing open his heart. 'I forgive you, Ammar.' *And I forgive myself.*

Ammar broke into a smile and started forward. Clumsily, because it had been so long, he reached to embrace Khalis. Khalis put his arms around Ammar, awkwardly, yet with a new and hesitant hope.

He couldn't have done it, he knew, without Grace. Without her strength. She'd been strong enough to walk away from him. And now he prayed she would come back to him when he found her.

Ammar stepped back, his smile as awkward as Khalis's hug. This was new and uncomfortable territory for both of them. 'It is good,' he said, and Khalis nodded.

'What will you do now?' he asked after a moment. 'Tannous Enterprises should by rights be yours.'

Ammar shook his head. 'Father wanted you to have it—'

'But I don't want it. And your whole life has been dedicated to the company, Ammar. Perhaps now you can make something of it. Something good.'

'Maybe.' Ammar looked away. 'If it is possible.'

'I'll sign my shares over to you—'

'I need to do something first.'

Surprised, Khalis blinked. 'What?'

'I need to find my wife.'

'Your *wife*?' He had not known his brother had married. But of course he had not known anything about these last fifteen years.

'Former wife, I should say,' Ammar corrected grimly. 'The marriage was annulled ten years ago.'

Curiosity sharpened inside him, but the hard set of his brother's features kept Khalis from asking any more probing questions. 'Still,' he said, 'you should take control of Tannous Enterprises. Turn it around, if you will.' Perhaps then the company could be redeemed, as Grace had suggested. Redeemed rather than dismantled and destroyed.

'There is time to discuss these matters,' Ammar said, and Khalis nodded.

'You must come to Alhaja. We can celebrate there.'

Ammar's mouth twisted. 'I've always hated that place.'

'As did I. But perhaps we can redeem even that wretched island.'

'You are full of hope,' Ammar observed wryly. He did not sound particularly hopeful himself. His brother might have changed, but he still looked haunted.

'I am,' Khalis answered. His heart felt light, lighter than ever before. He felt as if he could float. And he needed to find Grace. 'And while you need to find your wife, I need to find my—' He paused. 'My love.' Smiling, he embraced his brother once more. 'And tell her so.'

Six hours later, Khalis strode into the head office of Axis Art Insurers. A receptionist flapped at him, saying she'd have to check if Ms Turner was available, but Khalis just flashed her a quick smile and kept walking. Nothing was going to keep him from Grace now.

He'd wandered down several wrong corridors before he finally found her in one of the labs. She was standing in front of a canvas—he couldn't see what it was and, frankly, he didn't care—and his heart swelled with love at the sight of her. She wore a crisp white blouse and navy pencil skirt, reminding him of when he'd first seen her. Her hair was up in its classic chignon, but a few tendrils had escaped and curled around her neck. She gestured to the unseen canvas with one slender arm, and he felt pride swell along with overwhelming love. She was so strong. So amazing, to have come so far and done so much on her own. To have not just survived, but triumphed.

Khalis opened the door.

Grace heard the door open, felt that prickling along the nape of her neck that had alerted her to Khalis's presence before. Her body was wired to his in some elemental way, and yet…

Surely he couldn't be here.

He was. She turned and saw him looking as mouth-dryingly gorgeous as ever, his expression intent and serious as he gazed at her. And Grace gazed back, drinking him in, knowing that even though it had only been a few days she'd missed him. Terribly.

He nodded towards the canvas on the stainless steel table. 'Forgery?'

'No, it appears to be genuine so far.'

Khalis gave her a crooked smile. 'I don't know much about art, but thank God I know the real thing when I see it.' He closed the space between them in two long strides and swept her into his arms. 'You.'

Grace's arms came around him as a matter of instinct even as she searched his face. 'Khalis—'

'I found my brother. I talked to him.'

Her arms tightened around him. 'I'm glad.'

'So am I. Mainly because losing you over something like that would have killed me. But also because you were right. I did need to face my past. Face my family, and that darkness in myself.' His throat worked as his voice choked just a little. 'I needed to forgive myself.'

She laid one hand against his cheek. 'Sometimes that's the most difficult part.'

'But worth it. Most definitely worth it.' He bent his head and, smiling, Grace tilted her own back as he kissed her softly, a promise. 'Now,' Khalis said as he lifted his head, 'we really can look towards the future. Our future.'

'That sounds like a wonderful idea.' Grace's gaze widened when she saw him retrieve a small velvet box from his pocket.

'And I think,' Khalis said with a smile, 'it can begin with this. Grace Turner, will you marry me?'

She let out a shocked and joyous laugh. 'Yes. Yes, I will.'

'Then,' Khalis said, sliding a gorgeous diamond and sapphire ring onto her finger, 'the future looks very bright indeed.'

EPILOGUE

GRACE stared at the imposing villa in one of Athens's best neighbourhoods and felt a flutter of nerves so strong it was more like a kick in the gut.

'What if she's forgotten me?' she whispered. 'What if she doesn't want to go with me?'

Khalis slipped his hand into hers and squeezed. 'We'll take it together, one step at a time. One second at a time, if need be.'

Grace let out a slow breath and nodded. It had taken six months to get to this moment. Her ex-husband had been brought to court in a custody appeal, and after a lengthy trial Grace had been awarded main custody of Katerina, with Loukas having her every other weekend. Furious that he'd been thwarted, her ex-husband had relinquished all claims on his daughter. Even though Grace was saddened that he'd rejected Katerina, she was thrilled to have her daughter back. Thrilled and terrified. After years of stilted and unsatisfactory visits, she'd finally tuck her in at night. Sing her songs. Hold her close.

If Katerina would let her.

'I'm so scared,' she whispered and Khalis put his arm around her as he guided her up the front steps.

'The past really is the past,' he reminded her. 'We're looking towards the future now—as a family.'

A family. What a wonderful, amazing, humbling thought. Gulping a little, Grace nodded and pressed the doorbell.

Katerina's nanny answered the door; she had remained on as the child's carer while the trial went on. Now, with trepidation, Grace introduced herself and then waited as the nanny went to bring her Katerina.

The first sight of her daughter in several months nearly brought her to her knees. She'd grown several inches and, at nearly six years old, she was starting to lose some of that toddler roundness. Her eyes were wide and dark as she stared at Grace.

'Hello, Katerina,' Grace said, her voice only just steady. Khalis squeezed her hand in silent, loving encouragement. 'Hello, darling.'

Katerina gazed at her for a long moment, and then glanced at Khalis curiously before turning back to Grace. She offered a shy, hesitant smile. 'Hello, Mama,' she said.

* * * * *

ROMANCE

A Vow of Obligation	Lynne Graham
Defying Drakon	Carole Mortimer
Playing the Greek's Game	Sharon Kendrick
One Night in Paradise	Maisey Yates
His Majesty's Mistake	Jane Porter
Duty and the Beast	Trish Morey
The Darkest of Secrets	Kate Hewitt
Behind the Castello Doors	Chantelle Shaw
The Morning After The Wedding Before	Anne Oliver
Never Stay Past Midnight	Mira Lyn Kelly
Valtieri's Bride	Caroline Anderson
Taming the Lost Prince	Raye Morgan
The Nanny Who Kissed Her Boss	Barbara McMahon
Falling for Mr Mysterious	Barbara Hannay
One Day to Find a Husband	Shirley Jump
The Last Woman He'd Ever Date	Liz Fielding
Sydney Harbour Hospital: Lexi's Secret	Melanie Milburne
West Wing to Maternity Wing!	Scarlet Wilson

HISTORICAL

Lady Priscilla's Shameful Secret	Christine Merrill
Rake with a Frozen Heart	Marguerite Kaye
Miss Cameron's Fall from Grace	Helen Dickson
Society's Most Scandalous Rake	Isabelle Goddard

MEDICAL

Diamond Ring for the Ice Queen	Lucy Clark
No.1 Dad in Texas	Dianne Drake
The Dangers of Dating Your Boss	Sue MacKay
The Doctor, His Daughter and Me	Leonie Knight

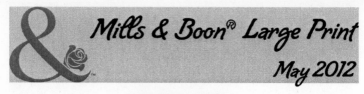

Mills & Boon® Large Print

May 2012

ROMANCE

The Man Who Risked It All	Michelle Reid
The Sheikh's Undoing	Sharon Kendrick
The End of her Innocence	Sara Craven
The Talk of Hollywood	Carole Mortimer
Master of the Outback	Margaret Way
Their Miracle Twins	Nikki Logan
Runaway Bride	Barbara Hannay
We'll Always Have Paris	Jessica Hart

HISTORICAL

The Lady Confesses	Carole Mortimer
The Dangerous Lord Darrington	Sarah Mallory
The Unconventional Maiden	June Francis
Her Battle-Scarred Knight	Meriel Fuller

MEDICAL

The Child Who Rescued Christmas	Jessica Matthews
Firefighter With A Frozen Heart	Dianne Drake
Mistletoe, Midwife...Miracle Baby	Anne Fraser
How to Save a Marriage in a Million	Leonie Knight
Swallowbrook's Winter Bride	Abigail Gordon
Dynamite Doc or Christmas Dad?	Marion Lennox

Mills & Boon® Hardback

June 2012

ROMANCE

A Secret Disgrace	Penny Jordan
The Dark Side of Desire	Julia James
The Forbidden Ferrara	Sarah Morgan
The Truth Behind his Touch	Cathy Williams
Enemies at the Altar	Melanie Milburne
A World She Doesn't Belong To	Natasha Tate
In Defiance of Duty	Caitlin Crews
In the Italian's Sights	Helen Brooks
Dare She Kiss & Tell?	Aimee Carson
Waking Up In The Wrong Bed	Natalie Anderson
Plain Jane in the Spotlight	Lucy Gordon
Battle for the Soldier's Heart	Cara Colter
It Started with a Crush...	Melissa McClone
The Navy Seal's Bride	Soraya Lane
My Greek Island Fling	Nina Harrington
A Girl Less Ordinary	Leah Ashton
Sydney Harbour Hospital: Bella's Wishlist	Emily Forbes
Celebrity in Braxton Falls	Judy Campbell

HISTORICAL

The Duchess Hunt	Elizabeth Beacon
Marriage of Mercy	Carla Kelly
Chained to the Barbarian	Carol Townend
My Fair Concubine	Jeannie Lin

MEDICAL

Doctor's Mile-High Fling	Tina Beckett
Hers For One Night Only?	Carol Marinelli
Unlocking the Surgeon's Heart	Jessica Matthews
Marriage Miracle in Swallowbrook	Abigail Gordon

ROMANCE

An Offer She Can't Refuse	Emma Darcy
An Indecent Proposition	Carol Marinelli
A Night of Living Dangerously	Jennie Lucas
A Devilishly Dark Deal	Maggie Cox
The Cop, the Puppy and Me	Cara Colter
Back in the Soldier's Arms	Soraya Lane
Miss Prim and the Billionaire	Lucy Gordon
Dancing with Danger	Fiona Harper

HISTORICAL

The Disappearing Duchess	Anne Herries
Improper Miss Darling	Gail Whitiker
Beauty and the Scarred Hero	Emily May
Butterfly Swords	Jeannie Lin

MEDICAL

New Doc in Town	Meredith Webber
Orphan Under the Christmas Tree	Meredith Webber
The Night Before Christmas	Alison Roberts
Once a Good Girl...	Wendy S. Marcus
Surgeon in a Wedding Dress	Sue MacKay
The Boy Who Made Them Love Again	Scarlet Wilson